DETECTIVE LAMBCHILD

The Court of Inquiry

M. LAWRENCE MOORE

ISBN
978-1-957895-34-5 (Paperback)
978-1-957895-33-8 (eBook)

TABLE OF CONTENTS

THE DETECTIVE

"Normally we would have discovered the body yesterday. We called your department today as soon as the children found this poor soul."

"You normally discover bodies on Tuesdays?"

Jean Patrice, the principal of the Center, studied her friend, the young detective.

"Yes. Every Tuesday," she said drily. "It was getting fairly monotonous."

"If you don't mind, could you walk me through what happened?"

"The students came here to their first class this morning and saw that their teacher was uncharacteristically punctual but dead. Yesterday was an inservice day for the faculty. No students."

"Why did you call homicide?"

"The note under her left hand says, 'I've been killed.' "

"Yes, I can see that now. Was she popular?"

"If it turns out that she was, in fact, murdered, I think the answer would have to be, mostly."

He thought about her response a moment. "I'll send for the crime scene people and the coroner and I will interview a few of your faculty this morning during their individual preparation periods. Did she have family?"

"No. In fact, I am listed on her employment record as her only emergency contact."

They walked out of the classroom together and the principal locked the door and took the key off a giant key ring next to her oversized rosary attached to her sash and handed it to him. "Please use my office for your interviews. As sad as this is, it is good to see you again, David David."

"Thank you, sister. By the way, what did she teach?"

"English. The students had just turned in their latest writing assignments."

"May I look at the students' papers?"

"Yes, but I hope you do not expect to find a confession."

"Maybe not a confession to murder."

<hr>

The crime scene investigators and the medical examiner had done their work and left and David David was alone in the classroom with a set of writing assignments from the decedent's class.

Fortunately, from his point of view, the students' papers were not polished, and the teacher's corrections afforded many examples of her handwriting to compare to the note that had been with the body. After ten minutes it was clear that the late Ms. Sanchez had not written the note. The pen that wrote the note was not in the room, either. After half an hour he decided that the handwriting did not match any of the students' papers and went in search of the class roll to see if there were any students who had not submitted the assignment.

Sister Jean Patrice was not available, but a really arrogant, angry assistant principal supplied him with the grade book which included the class roll. Two students had not turned in any work, but both had transferred out of state weeks before.

The assistant principal offered his opinion. "She referred to her class as 'devil's children.' There is one student in particular I think you should look at. His nickname is 'psycho Bobby'. He is really vile and capable of murder. "

David David thought this was very odd, but he did not say so to the vindictive assistant principal. Instead, he had a strong suspicion and asked him, "I really appreciate your help, but I have memory issues with names. Could you write down this Bobby's full name and address and anything else about him you feel is important? It might be very useful."

⸻ ✦✦✦✦ ⸻

Before leaving the Center's school, he located Sister Jean Patrice to return her classroom key.

"How attached are you to the assistant principal?"

"I will be very circumspect in my answer. I'm not.You should know that there are actually two schools. We share some faculty with the public school in the next block. The assistant principal works part of the time here at the Center's school which is tailored to the needs of its residents who are challenged. He resents the existence of this school and works actively to damage most of our students and those who have transferred to the regular grade school or high school.

He and his sister run an adoption agency with a terrible reputation. They have been investigated for selling children."

"O.k., I get all that. Who is 'psycho Bobby'?"

She was a very refined lady but her first reaction sounded like a small, resentful snort.

"Formerly known as 'psycho Bobby' he is now known as 'Bobby' or 'just Bobby', a resident of our center. He has made very slow, mostly steady progress and transferred to the regular high school more than a year ago. The assistant principal probably does not know that but immensely dislikes him. He targets certain students or entire classes and fabricates criminal charges to enforce his prejudices.

"The principal of the high school is a very fair man and would like to fire the assistant principal, but the law and order superintendent will not allow it, yet. Bobby's entire class is in danger of not graduating because of various charges and rumors instigated by this assistant. There is another student in that class named Christopher, nicknamed 'the disciple.' He is a loyal friend of Bobby. That may be why the assistant principal has gone after him and even had him arrested using false charges."

"I was told at the courthouse that a retired judge who is a friend of my family is substitute teaching at the high school. He's conducting a mock trial along the lines of one of his old courts of inquiry regarding exactly what you mentioned, why his entire class has been threatened with not graduating. That trial should take place in two weeks."

"I am meeting with the principal of the public school at about seven and if you are not busy, I think you will have a chance to meet him and Bobby, too. I will give you his address."

———— •·•✦✦•·• ————

David returned to the cold case squad room to handle the paperwork for this improbable homicide. He felt the case was solved, but it might involve some politics. The assistant principal was the nephew of the superintendent. The chief's saying came to mind that most things were not political problems if his detectives warned him ahead of time. He would come out of his office just before lunch and that would be a good time to brief him. David would do paperwork until then.

Meanwhile his cold case partner, Sue, had a mystery of her own. A message on her desk simply said, "The worm called." She had been with the squad five years longer than David, but she was totally baffled and asked for his help, so he asked her, "Which secretary would have the nerve and bitterness to leave you that note? Who could have made her so bitter? Why would she not be afraid that the chief would see it? She seems to think you will know who 'the worm' is."

Sue thought about it and said, "Oh. Oh! Thanks. How did you figure all that out?"

"I do my best thinking when I am thinking about two things at the same time."

The chief was a no nonsense leader. His office door was kept open so he could hear what was going on in the squad room. Just before lunch, the chief's voice, from his office, summoned his youngest detective. "Lambchild, in my office." The detective's immediate supervisor, Ed Johns, was already there.

"What about the teacher? Murder?"

"I'm sure not. The medical examiner will probably find her death was from natural causes. She was under the care of a heart doctor. She chose to die there, so she would not die unnoticed. Yesterday was an inservice day for the teachers at the Center. I think the time of death will show she went to the classroom soon after the final inservice meeting. There were graded papers on her desk with humorous corrections for the class which she called the 'devil's children.' A lesson plan on her desk was prepared for today. The pen that wrote the note was not with her. For his own reasons, an assistant principal wrote the note found under her hand, 'I have been killed,' possibly while she slept. His handwriting and ink from information I had him write match the note. If she was already dead, he could be charged with interfering with the police investigation by trying to implicate a student that he dislikes, but that would be hard to prove."

"I understand you are meeting with some other people this evening to finish up your investigation— without publicity, if possible." This last part indicated the chief felt David had matured since coming to his special squad and that he could be trusted to solve the case without sensationalism.

"Yes, sir. I am meeting the administrator for the Center and the principal of the nearby high school and the accused student named 'just Bobby'. I am told Bobby knows many people in law enforcement and knows many criminals from his parents' earlier connections."

"Between now and then, take the afternoon off. I don't want to pay you overtime." The chief was very fair and very tough but also could not come out and say thank you.

Sue came by after the chief left for lunch and said, "That's how he says congratulations for solving this case quietly and for patching things up between him and the mayor last year. Until your first case the mayor wanted this squad dissolved. Take his advice, enjoy the afternoon. Take my advice, go find somebody, somebody actually alive.

"By the way, a man who competed to get the job as our chief tried to get my secretary fired for being loyal to the chief. Even if he saw the note on my desk, the chief would probably know who wrote the note, the person she meant, and might even approve of the description."

+ + ♦ + +

There was only one place to go to enjoy himself— Arboretum Canyon. He would like that but did not see how he would meet anyone there.

The trail wound up one side of the canyon for half a mile, did a turnaround at the top and then back down the other side. There were native trees and grasses and bushes enough for anyone. There were turpentine bushes and alligator juniper and creosote that smells like rain when the leaves were crushed. Toward the top, just past a tree named sandpaper oak, was a mountain laurel with large clusters of purple flowers which really smelled like grape bubble gum. He had crossed over the top of the canyon called the saddle and was resting under an Arizona Ash. There was a flat, rock ledge half way below on his side of the canyon. He was so moved by the peacefulness and grandeur and harmony compared to his usual homicide work that he spoke out loud, "Such beauty. Such peace. And now, so ugly." In the shade of a mesquite tree the body of a young woman lay on the ledge where he presumed she had fallen.

Before descending the short distance to the body, he called 911, identified himself as Detective David Lambchild, and vented his frustration that, in the middle of all this nature, a young woman lay dead. "Everything was so pure and beautiful and now an ugly body."

"Mountain Rescue and Recovery is on the way."

"Who the hell do you think you're calling ugly?" She was alive, awake, and furious.

"I thought you were dead."

"And ugly."

"Only because you were dead. You really are beautiful in real life."

"This is the operator. You know we can still hear you."

"Thank you. Cancel."

"Are you sure? You might still need an ambulance."

"911, out." This time he made sure he had disconnected the call. He knew the operator and knew that he would never hear the end of his mistake.

"You did look so peaceful."

"So, I'm more pleasant dead?"

His phone rang and in the vast silence of the canyon she could hear a man's voice, "Your mother wants to know if you are joining us for dinner."

"May I bring a guest?"

Mrs. Lee said, "David will you say the grace?"

The guest was surprised when the father said grace rather than the son. The mother and father had their heads bowed, but when the father thanked God for the food as well as for their "beautiful guest," the beautiful guest gave their son a dirty look and he saw it and smiled.

Watching the enormous tension between his son and their guest brought some inexplicable inner joy to the father. The roast beef with mashed potatoes and brown gravy, the green beans, the salad were all excellent, the lemon meringue pie was perfect, but there was something more. After dessert, David David asked to be excused to change for his evening meeting with Sister Jean Patrice and the high school principal.

The father could contain himself no longer and simply said, "You have a question."

"Yes. How could two such lovely people raise anyone who thinks I'm ugly?"

Mrs. Lee was was partly defensive and partly amused, but Mr. Lee laughed so hard tears ran down his face and he dabbed them away with his cloth napkin. "David David came to us when he was five. He was an orphan and was being raised by a church congregation nearby. We had lost our teenage daughter the year before and they came to us. Our daughter had such passion, such fire, that I think we both wanted to be dead without her. David David has been a blessing, but we are getting older and he needs friends his own age."

Mrs. Lee made sure Mr. Lee was through and said, "We were almost too old to adopt; we call ourselves his grandparents. He is named after Mr. Lee and Mr. Lee's father but we kept the name the congregation called him as his last name."

David was back and had not changed out of his hiking clothes for his meeting after all. It finally occurred to him to ask, "Do you have a place to stay? I mean, I did find you sleeping in a canyon."

"Peacefully, until you came along and reported that you had found an ugly, dead body. And yes, I live with my parents a few miles from here. I walked to the arboretum. Any other questions?"

"Yes, two. What's your name?"

"Jillian."

He looked at her. With all his heart and soul, he knew. He knew. He even knew that he knew.

Kneeling beside her chair, "Jillian, if your parents don't object, will you marry me?"

"Do I get an engagement ring?"

Before he could answer, his mother put up her hand like a stop sign and within less than half a minute returned with her engagement ring and handed it to David who handed it to Jillian.

The father said, "Some very fast, very good decisions have been made in this room. Mrs. Lee and I agreed to adopt David in this room— even before we met him."

✦✦✦✦✦

David and Jillian agreed to stop by Mr. Scousin's before seeing her parents whom she had called. Bobby was approaching the front gate from the opposite direction coming from Giuseppe's restaurant and held the gate for them.

"You're Jillian Walsh. Your dad is the warden." "I'm Bobby, 'just Bobby' to my friends."

"I'm David David. Thanks for that piece of information."

Now on the porch, Jillian and David were introduced to the principal and Jillian to Jean Patrice. She asked Jillian if she knew anyone who could teach English.

"I will have my Education degree in May with English and History teaching fields."

"You could teach at the center with an emergency certificate this semester. David can give you the number. We'll talk tomorrow."

David said to Bobby, "Your teacher is the judge. He's having a court of inquiry in his classroom? I'm a witness."

"Me, too."

• • ♦ ♦ ♦ • •

"Mom, dad, this is David."

"Ma'am. Sir. I am happy to meet you. I am David David Lambchild."

It was very quiet in the Walsh living room for nearly twenty seconds. Sometimes that is a very long time. The husband and wife were holding hands. They were in perfect sync, watching their daughter and David. Finally, she squeezed his hand and the father said, "Do you have a ring?"

Jillian extended her closed left hand. It was cramped because she had not opened it since David put his mother's ring in it nearly an hour ago.

"Yes, sir, but we need your blessing."

With a glance at his wife who squeezed his hand again, he nodded and smiled.

David knelt and said, "Jillian Walsh, will you marry me?"

"Yes, I will marry you, David David."

———— ✦✦✦✦✦ ————

David was always half an hour early to work and still was not surprised that his immediate supervisor, Ed Johns, was already there. Half way through the morning, Ed Johns told David, "The chief wants to see us. The warden called."

David did not even have time to ask himself if Mr. Walsh had second thoughts about his approval yesterday.

"Congratulations."

"Thank you, sir." Apparently, the entire subject of yesterday was covered and concluded with the chief's one word. David thought they were through, but Ed Johns did not move toward the door so David waited.

"Lambchild. When I first heard your name from the mayor a year ago, I thought, at best, it was unfortunate. When I heard your grandmother had the opportunity to rename you at your adoption, I was sorry she missed her chance. This morning I met with a delegation from the Mount Shiloh Baptist Church on another matter and was reminded that the entire congregation had raised you until your adoption at age five. They reminded me that 'lambchild' is an old term reserved for a kind and gentle person. To belittle your name is to belittle them and that is not going to happen.

"Their visit concerns a child of the congregation named Alice. She is a crimefighter and is sometimes very helpful. She is a fifth grader and somehow was involved in a shooting at her school early this morning. This is not a cold case and is not in this precinct. You may be resented by the assigned detective. Fit in. Be tough.

"I know Alice from her tragic child abuse case. Also, she calls occasionally with information she thinks I can use. I want you to know more about Alice and whether someone shot at her and whether she is in danger. Dismissed."

<hr>

Detective Lambchild was directed to the classroom where the shooting occurred.

"Hello. I am Detective David Lambchild, and I was sent to assist in investigating the shooting and to meet Alice."

There were two patrolmen and a brusque detective named Brothers. He was clear about his animosity. No handshake. No greeting. "Sonny, we've got this covered. I've heard you are the mayor's darling and the chief's favorite and that you are practically clairvoyant, but you can go back and report that this case is very straightforward and is being handled without you. In fact, you can read in tomorrow's paper that a random act of violence against a fifth grader was thwarted by the courage of an assistant principal who was slightly wounded. He is the nephew of the school superintendent. He is receiving medical attention, but I interviewed him before he left. The officers interviewed the children of this class. They were taking a test and claim they saw nothing although three of them insist the assistant principal shouted in pain before he was shot.

"The fifth grader you are looking for is sitting in the assistant principal's office. Her back was to the shooter, but with your investigative skills, you might elicit who the shooter was. Another child was sent to the office for misbehaving earlier and is still there, also."

<hr>

David and his partner Sue went to the office. The chief had told him to have his partner Sue present for any interview with Alice. Before meeting her, they interviewed the boy who was in trouble for something apparently unrelated. He wanted to plead the fifth and say nothing without a lawyer, but the detectives told him that whatever he had done was probably unimportant compared to the other events of the morning. He was disappointed that his crime had been so cavalierly downgraded, so they decided to offer him immunity from prosecution in exchange for his information about what he had seen and heard. At first it was meant to be a joke but his information turned out to corroborate their next witness's story.

The boy explained he had heard the assistant principal yelling that someone had stolen his gold brick door stop and then he saw Alice walking after him with her metal lunch box, swinging it along her left side like a heavy pendulum. He thought he heard her say, "I've got your doorstop right here," but that made no sense to him. Sue wrote down what he had said and then told him to call his parents and have them take him home until tomorrow since school was being dismissed early because of the shooting.

Alice was in the assistant principal's outer office. Her metal lunchbox was resting on a chair and she was removing a standard sized brick, painted gold. She was using paper towels to handle it, possibly to avoid leaving fingerprints. She did not seem concerned that the police were watching her not leave fingerprints. Her thick glasses kept sliding down and she kept pushing them back to the bridge of her nose.

Sue started, "Hi, Alice. I'm Sue. Maybe you already know David David. Why are you still here? Everyone else has gone home."

"I knew you would come."

"Do you know Detective Lambchild?"

"Yes. Hi, lambchild. My lunchbox was too light to do any damage. That's why I needed the brick."

David nodded because that made sense so far.

"I saw on television that it really hurts if you hit someone on the front of his leg."

Another nod of agreement.

"I followed him to the classroom and hit his leg as hard as I could. That's why he yelled and fell on top of me and did not die from getting shot. The man from the ambulance said he was 'grazed and dazed.' "

David and Sue both stared at this eleven year old fountain of information with her thick, giant glasses. She was not through.

"Do you know why someone shot Mr. Rebele?"

It was Alice's turn to nod.

"When no one is listening he calls me Snow White." She extended her arm to show how black her skin was. "He laughs at Juice who cannot talk. He wrote a mean note to blame Bobby when my English teacher just died on her own. That's not why I hit him in the leg."

Wisely, they waited.

"He sold my friend, Danny, from his adoption business and it was not working so the buyer shot at him, but I messed it up. The buyer was making my friend, Danny, learn to shoot to make him a killer, but Danny is not like that. That is why the buyer wants you to think Danny shot Mr. Rebele, to get rid of Mr. Rebele first and later get rid of Danny."

"I could test your friend to see if he has fired a weapon before someone makes him shoot a weapon today."

"Yes. I thought of that.You must watch the same tv crime shows I watch. Danny is with Christopher, the disciple. I will find Christopher and he will bring Danny. The mean detective in the classroom thinks the assistant principal saved my life." Alice rolled her eyes to summarize everything she needed to convey on that topic.

David and Sue took Alice home to her parents who also knew him from the church and who also called him his original name, lambchild. They then returned to the cold case squad room. David called Jillian

Walsh and arranged to meet at her house later that evening. Then he asked Ed Johns, his immediate supervisor, for some help.

"About the shooting at the school?"

"Yes. I have a strange request. I met the detective in charge at the school, Detective Brothers. He really does not like me, but we can use that to solve the case."

"Someone doesn't like you? Normally, I would say solve your own social problems. The emergency operator said you did such a good job in the canyon."

"A boy named Danny is going to be framed as the school shooter. If the detective tests him for gunshot residue and he is clean now and tests dirty later today or tonight, the detective will look good and will be a perfect witness."

"Ok. I will call him and have him test the boy immediately as a possible shooter. Can we find the boy today?"

"Yes. A student named Christopher the disciple will deliver him immediately."

"You don't mind if I tell Detective Brothers that I don't like you either? That will make me more simpatico." Sue thought that was great.

They gave Ed Johns the family phone number for Alice and asked that she instruct Christopher the disciple to deliver Danny to Detective Brothers immediately. Alice found Christopher the disciple who delivered Danny to Detective Brothers within minutes in his huge, beautiful, clean, beige 1966 Chrysler Newport. Detective Brothers did not interview Danny but did test his hands and windbreaker for gunshot residue. Detective Brothers released Danny with really forceful instructions to tell no one about the test. He was delivered back to Christopher who dropped him near the house where he lived with his caregivers.

Mr. Stack, the adoptive father, had hired a couple to raise Danny while he was trying to train him to kill. That plan was such a disaster that he decided to kill the assistant principal and frame Danny and then kill Danny thus getting rid of any evidence of his plan. Alice wrecked the first part of that plan.

Within an hour of Danny's return to his residence, Mr. Stack contacted Detective Brothers. Mr. Stack said he understood Danny might be considered a possible suspect in the shooting of his friend, Mr. Rebele, the assistant principal. He emphasized Danny had no alibi during the time of the shooting, so he thought it was important that Danny be tested immediately for gunshot residue to exclude him and protect his rights. The detective told Mr. Stack he appreciated his concern and to bring Danny in right away but not to discuss the case with him.

Detective Brothers told Danny in front of Mr. Stack that he had the right to remain silent and he strongly urged the boy to do that during the test which now showed the boy had fired a weapon recently. The detective did not reveal that Danny was tested earlier or the results of either test.

Nonetheless, Mr. Stack acted saddened and very disappointed and left with Danny. Detective Brothers called Detective Lambchild. "You knew the boy would test clean the first time I tested him and dirty after Mr. Stack set him up?"

"Yes."

"You used me."

"Yes."

"That was good work, but I still don't like you."

"I know. I'm clairvoyant." Detective Brothers genuinely laughed."

Before his shift was over Detective Brothers got the call from Mr. Stack that he was expecting, asking about the results of the gunshot residue test.

Detective Brothers told him that normally he would not discuss the results but that he should prepare himself since the test was positive.

The detective asked who had trained Danny to shoot?

"I taught him but never to shoot a person. The caregivers and I are so disappointed.We've tried so hard with him."

"I think we can close this case if we can get the weapon he used to shoot the assistant principal, but I just don't understand his motive."

"Mr. Rebele and his sister actually arranged the adoption. Such an ungrateful child. I know where Danny keeps the pistol. I will not touch it, but I will take you to it. I suppose there may be fingerprints. I heard Mr. Rebele survived. I hope he is all right."

"He suddenly bent forward just before he was shot, so he was grazed down the back of his skull and all the way down his back. Very Painful. He also suffered an injury to the front of his right leg somehow. We were told this morning that he bent down to shield a little girl from the shooter and that's what saved his life."

"What a wonderful man."

———— ·+++++·+ ————

Meanwhile, David and Jillian were spending that same evening learning more about each other and about each other's families with long, peaceful pauses between the narratives. They were sitting on her parents' front porch swing.

Jillian spoke of being partly frightened and partly excited about teaching. She spoke of helping the class mourn the loss of a teacher they loved. As a tribute to their late teacher, Ms. Sanchez, she had received permission from the class to continue calling them devil's children.

David spoke of Alice whose lunchbox assault was the talk of the squad room. He spoke of Alice's friend Danny who was not actually sold by the Rebeles to Mr. Slack but said a worse adoption placement would have been hard to imagine.

—————— ·•✦✦✦•· ——————

Detective Brothers was in the cold case squad room the next morning and much nicer to David Lambchild who had steered him in the right direction and stayed in the background. Ed Johns thanked him for allowing Sue Lacy and David Lambchild on his turf.

"They did a good job, but actually their other partner, Alice, deserves a lot of the credit. You know something odd. Despite the blood and injury on the assistant principal's right leg, her metal lunchbox was tested and was totally negative for his blood or DNA."

David knew she had switched lunch boxes but let Ed Johns tell him. "She has an extra, a throw down lunch box. She watches crime shows on television."

Sue told Brothers, "The article in the news is a good diversion. The shooter will think you are considering Danny as the shooter." She knew that was exactly what he thought at first.

The chief came onto the squad room and acknowledged Detective Brothers then said to David, "Former Judge David Howell has arranged for a court of inquiry to be conducted in his classroom next week. I understand you originally were being called as a witness regarding circumstances surrounding the death of the English teacher, Ms. Sanchez, at the Center. You may still testify that the teacher's death has been ruled natural and your affidavit regarding the death and the note will probably then be accepted by the court.

"The assistant principal has also been called as a witness to testify regarding what he knows about efforts to prevent this class from graduating. Before his injuries he had protested to the school board about participating. I am told he is the main source of efforts to block this class from graduating. He may be asked if he wrote the note found beside the teacher and whether he suggested that a particular student had killed Ms. Sanchez.

"The attorney for the school district called me with the latest developments. Now a sitting district judge, Judge Villa, has convened the court which is now legally constituted. It will focus on whether the students' right to an education have been interfered with in violation of federal law.

"Normally, your assignments are cold case homicides and occasionally current homicides. I have authority to assign you to investigate any illegal activity and have been requested to do so by Judge Villa. Detective Brothers will continue to handle the shooting and will call on us if he needs to. I would like our involvement in school legal matters minimized. I want you to help Detective Brothers find the shooter and protect all the children including Alice.

"Before the beginning of the court of inquiry, you are to find out who "the disciple" is, whose disciple he is, and whether he is committing any crimes. You will find out his source of income and whether it is legal. If so, leave it at that. Has he been the subject of false reports and false arrests? You can turn that over to the assistant district attorney who will be part of the court of inquiry.

"Find out more about psycho Bobby and whether he is accused of any crimes, excluding the murder he was falsely accused of. I worked with Judge Howell during Bobby's placement at the Center. He knows most of the criminals and law enforcement in town and knows Warden Walsh.

"Find out about Adam, last name unknown, in the same class. Speak to his probation officer and find who pushed to raise his bond from personal recognizance to $30,000.00 and who posted that amount of money for a high school student from a lower middle income family.

"As a sideline the assistant principal and his sister run an adoption agency which is being federally investigated. Alice, the fifth grader you interviewed yesterday, called me and said she wants me to know you are doing a good job. She said she has information regarding how she can identity of the shooter and who is next. She wants to talk to you.

"Former Judge Howell and now Judge Villa have agreed the court of inquiry will still last no more than one hour."

THE DISCIPLE

While helping her second grade class recite their phonics (today's drill was consonant blends), the teacher watched the entire class but him very closely trying not to be obvious. He sat in the second chair, middle row. It was afternoon but for the entire morning and again now he sat mashed against the metal brace on the right side of his heavy wooden desk all the while doing the work assigned including participating in the phonics recitation. He was left-handed so his slightly contorted position in his desk chair did not prevent him from printing his letters. Ms. Sally was a tough disciplinarian, and if this were misbehavior, it would be easy to handle. She saw that it was not.

There was no indication of discomfort. If he needed the restroom he could have asked throughout the morning or gone at lunchtime. Nonetheless, she finally could not stand it and signaled for Christopher to approach her huge metal desk eight feet from the nearest student's desk.

She was reluctant to speak to him. There was a reserve about him. She knew almost every family of every student. The exception was Christopher. Normally, as each student checked in, she or the school staff had some interaction with at least one parent. Christopher was always the first child to arrive, alone at a nearly empty school. He would pick up trash on the playground and then go wash up usually before anyone including staff arrived. After school he helped one or the other of the janitors until the staff lost interest in meeting his parents and he just went home.

She spoke so that only Christopher could hear. "Do you need to go to the restroom?"

"No, ma'am."

"Do you feel ill?"

"No, Ma'am."

We are running out of questions here, buddy. "Why are you sitting on only half your chair?"

"So my guardian angel can sit down. Yesterday, after church Sister told my friend Bobby and me that we each have a guardian angel. He must get very tired." Thinking about someone showing him unending love and close attention, he almost started crying, but Ms. Sally prevented that as she had been taught in her education class by being just a little tough.

Ms. Sally was teaching with an emergency certificate meaning she did not get much money, but she wanted to keep her job by not getting into his religion in this public school.

"Guardian angels do not need to sit. You've seen balloons that float, they float. They cannot sit."

She thought about his church, her church, with its tall, very thick adobe walls, stuccoed and whitewashed outside and plastered inside. Pine log roof beams called vigas stretched from one side of the long, narrow church to the other. The church was still run by the Franciscans whose order of priests built a string of mission churches along the Rio Grande hundreds of years ago.

The next day Christopher was sitting in his desk like everyone else, but he had attached a length of heavy string to the metal support brace on his desk. Ms. Sally would rather die than ask but suspected it was in case his guardian angel wanted to anchor himself to avoid floating away.

• • ◆ ◆ ◆ • •

Ms. Sally got her teaching certificate and eventually taught Christopher and his friend Bobby one year at the high school. She saw that things were much the same for him. He was fiercely loyal. His first and best friend was Bobby from the Center. They still attended catechism after church on Sunday and were in the same classes when Bobby finally transferred from the Center to the regular high school. Because of his past, Bobby had occasional major problems,but Christopher stood by him and saw Bobby make slow, mostly steady progress. The assistant principal did not like either of them and tried to harm them.

Christopher was still idealistic and reserved. He was very protective of his mother and kept her away from the school. He figured out how to register himself on the computer in the school library for his freshman and sophomore year as the school allowed. Since the seventh and eighth grade were on the same campus, students who graduated from the campus eighth grade could automatically register on line without a parent appearing. Small problems started in his sophomore year, but by senior year confrontations with the assistant principal, Mr. Rebele, were inescapable. He thought it was because he let his guard down, but the problem was caused by this man who was supposed to be helpful.

In his sophomore year he started picking up aluminum cans to buy the smaller things his mother needed. He knew the regular size aluminum beer and soda cans were worth about three to four cents each and the sixteen ounce cans were worth seven. He happened to know that aluminum ore called bauxite partly came from Guinea and that instability there had raised the price of the cans he picked up to recycle. He had to discipline himself not to watch people finish their sodas and not to be obvious about memorizing where they discarded the cans. On Saturdays he would go to the metal monster carrying a black plastic trash bag that no one could see through to turn his crushed cans into small amounts of cash and then to the stores with the word "dollar" in their names to buy small things his mother needed with his very limited resources.

The metal monster was great because there were no humans and so no judgment about his poverty and no criticism. He would put in the crushed cans, get the receipt and the money. At the dollar store, the checkout clerk would ask for his phone number and he would blush every time. It was a ritual. Each time the clerk would say, "I'm not asking you out, I need your number for our records." His response was always the same, "No phone, ma'am."

In the late fall of his senior year as happens every fall the first hard freeze caused the green outer jacket of the pecan to spread open and allow the pecan, still in its brown shell, to fall or be shaken loose. He learned from an elderly man in his neighborhood that he could contract to pick up pecans from under the trees of residential owners and he would be paid ninety cents at the feed store for a full five-gallon bucket of unshelled pecans. Each tree owner received an agreed percentage of the profits.

It was fairly hard work. The neighbor was too old to work any more, but he helped Christopher obtain five-gallon plastic buckets from a place that sold hamburgers. Christopher cleaned the entire store property in exchange for four five-gallon pickle buckets. He invested under a dollar for a box of baking soda to get rid of the pickle odor. The manager at the hamburger stand was impressed with Christopher's ambition and manners. He told Christopher that a teaspoon or two of pickle juice would cure hiccups. Christopher stored that information away for later.

The retired neighbor took him to each of the pecan tree owners he had worked for and introduced Christopher and recommended him. The old man made sure each owner kept the contract the same, fifty/fifty. The lawyer across from the school was an exception. He had four trees but was allergic to pecans. He told Christopher to keep all the proceeds. To thank the old neighbor who got him his jobs, he gave half the proceeds from the lawyer's trees to him.

Christopher spent an entire day on the pecan farm where his helpful neighbor had worked when he was younger. The neighbor introduced him to the owner who introduced him to his sons. Christopher recognized them because their large family sang at his church back in town every Saturday night. In fact they were the entire choir. The boys were busy with the harvest but still managed to show him around.

The big orchard owners have or borrow machines with extended rubber forks which gently clamp the trunk of the tree and vibrate most of the pecans loose. The pecans land on the smoothly swept soil under the tree to be picked up by another machine with cylindrical brushes. Christopher watched the conveyor carry the pecans still in their brown shells into large wagons after separating out most of the leaves and twigs the brushes also swept up. Hiring people to pick up pecans from the ground is only marginally profitable for the orchard owners. Until the border fence was built, large numbers of people crossing the farm from Mexico or Central America would cut through the orchard and would leave their shoe indentations in the soft, swept soil. When the pecans landed there, they could not be swept up by the machines and cost extra to be picked up by hand. The family mostly avoided public comments about immigration or the border fences or about drug smuggling.

He learned about more than pecans that day. The sons told him of a brazen bar owner from Caseta named "the rabbit." He had left a small amount of drugs on the tailgate of their father's pickup one night with a note that said he would transport drugs through the farm when he liked and not to bother to contact Border Patrol or the relatives in Mexico of their father's workers would be used as an example of his cruelty. Each mid level smuggler packed his drugs in his own way like a signature. An elderly neighbor received three samples of differently packed drugs to show that the bar owner was not just local but was cartel affiliated, a connection the bar owner would greatly regret within weeks of Christopher's farm visit.

Christopher was not cursed with good looks, genius, or charm. In compensation he had the drive of an army of workers and he was humble, honest and wise. Utilizing these gifts, Christopher made enough to help his mother with something left to buy his own clothes at the Dollar General. He also bought a set of hair clippers. Most of the clothes for sale were dark colors and baggy. Those purchases were where the problem at school really started.

The principal of the school was a very tough, wise man. One of the teachers quietly referred to Mr. Skousin as "Mr. Shalom." Peacefulness and fairness were the rule. If he had not decided an issue, it was often settled the way he would settle it even if he never heard about it. Unfortunately, Mr. Skousin was out of the office for two months for surgery and recovery. The assistant principal saw this time as an opportunity to clean up the school, to shore up some discipline which he felt had long been neglected, to impress his uncle, the superintendent.

Throughout his sophomore and junior year, Christopher avoided the assistant principal as much as possible. In his senior year, when Mr. Skousin was out for two months, Christopher was without the protection of the principal.

This assistant principal, based on Christopher's short haircut and dark clothes and "sudden money," decided that he was in a gang and making money selling drugs. Christopher was ordered to bring his mother to the school for a meeting with the assistant principal and with a counselor. Meanwhile, a pistol had been stolen from near the school from a federal marshall's car where it was never supposed to be left. The report to the marshall's superior falsely stated that the Glock and identification and badge were all stolen from the marshall's house. An agent would be reprimanded for leaving his weapon in a vehicle but not for a burglary of his house.

A rumor had supposedly come to the attention of the assistant principal that one of the gangs had obtained the Glock. The assistant principal claimed that Christopher was probably involved and that he needed protection at the meeting with Christopher and his mother, so he called the police and suggested Christopher was the one most likely to bring the missing handgun to school.

SWAT was waiting when Christopher and his mother approached the school. His mother did not speak a word of English and therefore did not obey when the officers yelled for her to raise her hands and face the chainlink fence surrounding the school. Risking his life to protect her, Christopher told his mother in Spanish, "I always obey you. Please, this one time trust me and obey me. Put your hands against the fence and we will be safe."

There were red laser dots all over Christopher's face and jacket from the rifles of the SWAT marksmen. He knew what was at the other end of each laser. He bowed formally and humbly to the swat officers like at the start of a karate match then he laid down on the sidewalk and put his hands behind his head although the officers were still mostly shouting at his mother. The officers approached and cuffed him and lifted him up and pushed him against the chainlink fence and searched him. Nothing. The drug dog had no complaint against him either and there was no handgun, but the assistant principal charged Christopher with belonging to a gang and used the same short haircut, baggy, dark clothes and evidence of new money as probable cause. Unfortunately, the school resource officer did as he was told and signed a sworn complaint as instructed by the assistant principal charging Christopher with gang membership.

Normally, a person charged with a Class C offense of the state's education code receives a citation and notice to appear in court. Most other violations on school grounds have been decriminalized and reclassified as non-criminal, school business. The legislature had recently mandated that schools should be run by the schools, not the courts. Gang membership, however, was still considered a non-school matter, still a chargeable offense. State law left the decision to ticket or arrest anyone 17 or older in the discretion of the issuing officer. In this case, the officer was ordered by the assistant principal to arrest Christopher who was now 17.

The complaint had the statutory language, "In the Name and by the Authority of the State of Texas.The affiant (the one signing below) has reason to believe and does believe that on this day and on days prior to this the defendant did belong to a gang... Against the peace and dignity of the State."

Really tired of a barrage of illegal, ex-parte phone calls by the assistant principal lobbying for various convictions and for law and order in the schools, the judge asked, "Officer, does this young man really belong to a gang?"

"No, judge."

"Then why did you sign the complaint swearing that was true?"

"The assistant principal ordered me to."

"I am giving you two orders: One, never sign a false statement; that is false swearing, a crime. Two, go read about the trials at Nuremberg that followed World War II. Every Nazi that said he was just following orders was hanged for war crimes. After you read about it tell your assistant principal what you found out.

"Not guilty, young man. Please wait in the jury box until I finish this next matter, an arraignment."

The prosecutor was present and agreed with the not guilty finding, agreeing in effect that the judge's brief exchange with the officer constituted a short but complete trial. Otherwise, a dismissal could be refiled as a new case by the enthusiastic assistant principal.

Christopher recognized the student now before the judge from his auto repair class. He was originally charged with possession of something which Christopher had never heard of from a Penalty Group that fortunately Christopher also had never heard of. Early last night, at the urging of the assistant principal, the student was arrested for failure to report to his probation officer. He had apparently been up all night because of his arrest and yawned in the judge's face. The judge looked at the paperwork and then at the prisoner and, in an encouraging tone, said, "Don't do that, you will make me sleepy, too."

"I am sorry, I didn't realize."

The judge told the prisoner his rights, reinstated his personal recognizance bond which he did not have to do, and had him escorted out to prepare him for release. Then he called Christopher back before the bench. He removed his black robe and adjusted his tie and then sat back down perhaps to show this was not a part of the formal legal process. He asked Christopher if he could speak Spanish. His response was an idiom which translates, how could it be otherwise? "Como que no?"

"It is eleven-thirty. I have asked the deputy sheriff to let you call your mother at her work and then to give you a ride back to school in time for lunch. On the way he will stop at my friend's garage. His name is Homer.

He is expecting you. He restores cars and has a proposal for you. He only speaks Spanish. Good luck to you."

The deputy who took him back to school told other officers how Christopher had protected his mother first and then bowed to the officers. In time they would know Christopher for themselves, but this was a good start.

From day to day the school lunches ranged from incredible to inedible depending on who was cooking, but after hearing Homer's proposal, his mind was not on food. This preoccupation at first prevented him from noticing a difference in a few people at the school.

Despite the court's dismissal there was a change in how a some people looked at him. Some students and teachers who did not really know him began to see him differently. He still had no phone or computer so he could not be tormented by anyone on the internet, but that afternoon he heard those few whisper, "gangsta" or "measles" because of the laser dots incident, he supposed. A few teachers thought it might be true that he was a gang member because of how he looked and because SWAT does not come to the school for innocent students. Ms. Sally knew him and saw the SWAT incident and was enraged at the injustice.

The assistant principal encouraged the injustice and disparaged the soft judge who had found Christopher not guilty. Gang member wannabes called "peewees" were sent that afternoon to test him for possible membership. He was not interested or intimidated which made the higher ups in various gangs think his calm demeanor indicated he was already a gang leader.

Christopher was unsophisticated, simple. This incident could have caused him to lose all faith. If anything, it seemed that his faith was strengthened. He simply believed in the will of God and believed he needed to pray to know what that will was. His mother told him to go to church.

Early the next morning he sat quietly in one of the simple pine pews, worn and polished by several hundred years of use. The long, narrow church was lit only by the stand of votive candles nearby, each lit candle representing a parishioner's prayer. After an hour he was at peace and knew what to do, but consulted with his customer, the attorney.

To make sure he was not on school property, Christopher knelt on the lawn of the attorney, across the street from the school entrance and prayed with the blessing and permission of the attorney. He was wearing his dark plaid jacket and his navy blue, slightly baggy cotton pants, both fairly new and both purchased from the dollar store.

When Christopher entered the school, he was still on time, early in fact. He was met by his nemesis, the assistant principal, who ordered the school officer to file a complaint for criminal trespass for being in the yard of the school's neighbor. He told the resource officer, "We don't want trouble with the neighbors, especially that one, since he is an attorney."

The officer recalled the judge's instructions and told the assistant principal he had been ordered to sign only complaints he knew to be true but that he could prepare an affidavit or complaint for the assistant principal to sign and file. Further, he told the assistant principal, "I just received a note from the homeowner saying that he is Christopher's attorney and that he has given him permission to be in the yard."

The following day three seniors and a teacher, Ms. Sally, joined him on the lawn for a few minutes of silent prayer. The young lady he recognized from his church, her brother he recognized from auto class and from court. He was the one being taken before the judge when Christopher was there for his false gang affiliation charge. Stephanie and Adam.

The third senior was his friend, "just Bobby." He was formerly known as "psycho Bobby" through most of grade school. He lived at a private residential center nearby but now attended the same high school as Christopher. He walked alone to the entrance of the school. They attended the same religious classes after mass on Sunday along with the only black student in their school, Alice who was in the fifth grade.

Alice was actually Baptist but attended the same religious classes after her own Mt. Shiloh Baptist Church service ended. So far, no explanation was ever requested or offered. As a result of being thrown from a second story onto concrete when she was two, Alice had a pronounced limp and very thick glasses. Her truly dedicated adoptive parent had nursed her through the egg shell fracture of her skull. The swelling of her brain caused some nerve damage resulting in weakness on her left side when she got tired. Her optic nerve was also damaged, thus the need for thick glasses. Understandably, she also had a fierce law and order attitude with a burning desire to become a detective like her Baptist congregation's favorite son, Detective Lambchild.

They were all true friends even back when Bobby was "psycho Bobby." Bobby could always check with Christopher or Alice to see if something he thought he had experienced was real or a delusion. Christopher or Alice would separate fact from fantasy, tell the story back to Bobby, and never mention it again.

While the others were crossing the street in front of the school, the first young man said, "You probably don't recognize me without my handcuffs. My name is Adam. I was in court when you were. The judge allowed me out on bond again to finish the school year but I might get three months in the county jail after that for my probation violation— failure to report. Will you be here again tomorrow?"

"Yes, for the rest of the week. I want the school to know that I am not a bad person. I think that is my assignment."

This statement sounded strange to Adam but seemed to strengthen his first impression of Christopher as an advertisement for decency. "I brought my sister Stephanie and joined you because you look like you are at such peace."

— ✦✦✦✦ —

Homer came to his house the very next evening and spoke to Christopher's mother about his plan, then asked to speak to Christopher, also. The three agreed that Christopher would work after school three days a week and would be paid minimum wage until he was certified as a mechanic through his school classes. Homer invited the mother and Christopher to travel on Saturday to Sierra Blanca, about ninety miles east for the Hudspeth County Sheriff's annual auto auction to execute Homer's second proposal. He would explain more on the trip.

Homer drove his car hauler which could carry two cars. He was interested in one particular car which he called a bombita. It was from the 50's and needed work but would be valuable and would be displayed in regional car shows when restored. It had been abandoned on the small town's main street about eight months ago. The owner signed it over to the sheriff for storage fees and for a fine he owed the town. Probably no one else would bid on it since it required some skill to restore. Homer had already ordered the rich, royal blue paint in anticipation. This area of far West Texas was so dry there was almost no rust.

The car hauler was not uncomfortable. Lupe sat on the passenger side and Christopher sat in the middle of the bench seat and occasionally had to move himself out of the way of the stick shift located on the floor of the truck's cab. Christopher was curious about the second proposal of Homer's but was patient and silent.

The trip itself was interesting. Going on I-10 East out of El Paso, Lupe and Christopher could see several miles below to the right. A mile of sand and brush stopped suddenly at the railroad tracks and then just below the tracks — the highway known as Texas 20. The old road curved quite a bit, past the historic missions of Ysleta, Fabens, and Socorro, and past the town of Tornillo where the briefly famous tent city was located that housed the young men separated from their families by the immigration policy. Past that, also to the right, were pecan orchards and fields of alfalfa and cotton and onions and more, all irrigated by a series of canals and ditches. The farms in Mexico in the far distance grew many of the same crops and irrigated the same way. The pecan farm he had visited recently during the harvest was toward the end of the farms and only the pecan treetops were visible from the freeway. He could not actually see the metal fence separated the two countries. The farmer told him one thing he would not miss was a sign at a market in the little Mexican town very nearby advertising pecans for sale which proudly stated they were from his farm although they were not paid for.

The farmers whose land was directly against the Mexican border used to walk over small wooden bridges that crossed the canal and into the Mexican town. The doctor, located in a town called Guadalupe, once a great convenience to the valley farm population, disappeared along with his nurse after tending to a person wounded by drug dealers.

The American farmers receive a certain number of irrigation opportunities each year depending on the water level in Elephant Butte Lake in southern New Mexico. That lake depended on rain and snow in parts of Colorado and Northern New Mexico, the beginning of the Rio Grande. Homer said he would not explain the international water treaty which controlled the water disbursement except to say it included Colorado, New Mexico, Texas, the Mexican Government and the United States Government. This year the farmers who had wells were forced to use them since Elephant Butte Lake was so low. They had to be very careful since the well water would burn the pecan tree roots if it got salty and the aquifer the wells depended on was not limitless. This year they would get fewer irrigation opportunities to use river water which was not salty. Some farmers were investigating the cost of miniature desalinization systems based on the huge plant built by Fort Bliss and the City along the Montana highway. Its top output was about 25 million gallons of water per day, but it was very expensive. There was still the salt brine to dispose of.

After leaving the farm area there were very small communities with names from the Old West such as Fort Hancock, but eventually both sides of the freeway were sparsely filled with desert landscaping such as yucca and cactus and creosote and sage and many types of grass with red sand in between. No trees. No nada as some locals said.

About fifteen miles before their destination the car hauler began to climb toward what appeared to be an impassable mountain. The interstate seemed to disappear at the top of the mountain. At the beginning of this climb their vehicle slowed considerably and Homer obeyed the signs that ordered vehicles to travel in the right lane unless passing. The wind was very strong all the way up this slope. It did not move the car hauler but the noise was loud.

Homer pointed at a long sprawling set of white buildings on the right previously known as Tommy's and pointed out a faded sign advertising the Tiger Truck Stop. It was once a national chain with someone's idea to have at least one real tiger at each truck stop. Homer told how once he had watched calves grazing near the very long tiger's cage at the back of the truck stop. The tiger stalked the calves but of course could not get to them. There was an enormous deputy from Fort Hancock who had wrestled with two tiger cubs there until they began to see him as food rather than as a playmate. The tigers were gone, so Homer used the rest of the steep climb to set the stage for his second proposal.

He explained as they drove past the communication antennas at the very jagged tops of these mountains and through the nearly invisible winding pass at the top that the road would level off and they would come to a Border Patrol check point about five miles before the town. They would each have to declare their citizenship as "American" to the Border Patrol agent or possibly to an American soldier assisting the Border Patrol. He told them that one of the other functions of the checkpoint was to stop the flow of drugs. If the drug dogs alerted to a car or truck it was sent to a secondary station for an inspection. Homer said many of the cars at the auction were confiscated at this checkpoint since they had been used in the commission of the crime of transporting illegal drugs. Some cars had so much debt that they were not worth auctioning and would probably be turned over to the lien holder, the one who held the debt.

Homer told the mother and son about a second car, a '66 Chrysler Newport, as if just in casual conversation. He mentioned that if someone wanted to buy it, he could loan that person the money and keep half that unnamed person's wages each week as payment. Homer said that this vehicle was usually fairly good on gas mileage but that this particular car was really not according to his cousin but thought the problem was something small. He explained that all the sales were "as is" and if the car was worthless, the buyer was stuck.

They were waived through the checkpoint by a pleasant soldier who decided they were citizens which was true and that they were not a threat or smuggling drugs, also true. Now he had to crunch the rest of his second proposal into the five miles left before Sierra Blanca.

Homer said he had been contacted about the car he was discussing. Afterwards he called his cousin Raul, a Hudspeth County deputy, who gave him the background of this car. It had very low mileage and had been bought by a bar owner from just over the border from the son of an elderly person who had had to give up driving. The buyer was called "La Coneja" (the rabbit) and was a known drug smuggler. Normally rabbit is "El Conejo," but since he had given himself the nickname, everyone simply called him that. His employee or "mule" was a giant named Tiny who was caught with a load of marijuana in the Chrysler Newport at the Border Patrol checkpoint they had just left. Christopher had heard about La Coneja but did not interrupt.

The car was impounded and Tiny spent several weeks in the jail. The food was cooked by deputy Raul's mother and was the best in town. Tiny ate the food and did not lose weight but was insulted and furious that La Coneja and his superiors would not bond him out. The prosecutor risked being fired for giving Tiny probation in exchange for his statements to federal investigators without first seeking permission. Tiny told about the bar owner and his organization and about how the marijuana was kept in law enforcement evidence lockers in Mexico until time for transport.

Partly as a result of Tiny's evidence, the bar owner was federally indicted in five states and would not be returning to the United States or reclaiming this car. Sadly, Tiny tried to smuggle another load in another car after his release and shot at law enforcement and was in turn shot and killed. The bar owner's sponsors were so displeased that La Coneja had lost a second load, they shot his small bar to pieces. "The rabbit" disappeared.

Raul told Homer that he had personally moved this Chrysler twice within the vast impound lot. He tried to get drug dogs to "hit" on the car without success. Homer finished his story while pulling into the yard of the Hudspeth County sheriff's dirt impound lot which held several dozen cars for the potential buyers who were gathering.

Christopher was not eighteen. In Texas he was old enough to be arrested as an adult but not old enough to enter a legally binding contract. His mother had to put the car in her name. Ironically, when Homer and Christopher's mother went into the sheriff's office, the odor of marijuana was almost overwhelming. All evidence was stored in a huge closet within the office itself. It was most secure since the office was within the jail. They were at the western tip of West Texas which is extremely dry. This sheriff's office was an exception. If the marijuana dried out before trial, charges would have to be lowered if the weight dipped below the minimum weight for a particular crime class. The sheriff's solution was to keep the drugs humidified with an evaporative cooler in the extreme heat of the summer or, as now, with a humidifier. When his mother came back to the fenced impound area where he was studying the Chrysler, Christopher was shocked that his mother smelled like marijuana and not just barely.

Although the car had obviously been garaged most of its life and although it had ridiculously low mileage and brand new tires, no one else bid on this car, and his mother, Lupe, paid the sheriff of Hudspeth County $600.00 using Homer's money. Homer calculated that Christopher would pay the car off including tax, title, and license within three months from his part-time salary.

Christopher and his mother had never even been in a car this nice. It was beige and nearly the same color as the dust and sand which thickly coated it.The upholstery was a heavy nylon weave and like new. The steering wheel was huge. There were no plastic parts. He wanted to start it, but knew that it had sat for months. Cars from the 60's would require removing the giant air filter cover and pouring a little gas into the carburetor probably more than once to prime the engine. He and Homer both wanted to get it on Homer's transport behind Homer's faded, royal blue bombita and get home. Plus, Christopher did not have insurance or a driver's license yet. What would have been the point? But now...

The small adobe house where Christopher lived with his mother had a very long driveway leading to a brick garage. Homer slowly backed his car transport to line up with this driveway and very slowly lowered the Chrysler. They pushed the car to the back of the property and into the garage. It was too late tonight but tomorrow after church this car would be as clean as it was on the day it was made. He considered it but honestly did not think cleaning his car would be working on Sunday and so would not violate the commandment to keep the Sabbath holy.

Until now there was not much need for tools. Suddenly Harbor Freight and the car parts stores became very important. Homer had spoken less on the trip home but said he could loan Christopher tools from his shop now since he knew where he lived and worked.

The next morning Christopher saw Stephanie at church and they walked in the direction of both their houses. She spoke of her brother's drug addiction and how great he was when clean.

Christopher asked if Adam would mind her talking about this and she said, "He told me to tell you, to protect you."

Christopher thought about that. Stephanie told him that Adam had been kicked out of catechism class several years ago when a prior teacher had said, "Let us pray," and Adam had innocently said, "Spray what?" She said he just never went back to class or church but read the Bible. Christopher remembered the incident.

She lived closer to the church than he did, so he walked her to her door and still got home in time for lunch. His mom had been to the Spanish mass very early and had then made red cheese enchiladas. They were just out of the oven. Some said they were even better when reheated the next day. Christopher told his mother that his decision about which was better might require more research.

Fortified for his car project by his substantial lunch, he went to the shelf near his exercise area in the brick garage for his supplies. Wax was not recommended for newer cars with a clear coat to protect the paint, but this car was made and painted long before that idea. He took the can of wax Homer had given him and considered the cloth.

One of his schoolmates, Alice, called him school zone because he thought things out slowly. She flashed through his mind, and he whispered a tiny prayer for his friend, but that did not speed his decision.

This required a wardrobe decision. His wardrobe decisions reflected his character. His mother worked at a hotel cleaning rooms for minimum wage, but she also needed whatever he could make with his small jobs just to pay the groceries and utilities. When he occasionally needed to shave, he made lather from slivers of the tiny bars of used soap his mother brought home. He did his own laundry so that she would not see and worry about the condition of his underclothes. Once fully dressed for school he was always presentable although he could almost put his socks on from either end and he often wore his better t-shirt over one that was frayed or had holes.

The t-shirt being considered for final demotion to a wax rag he wore for exercising. It had been first been demoted to winter wear because of the holes. He wore it under other clothes as long as the collar was presentable. Now even that was frayed and too worn for public use. He admitted it was hardly worth putting on even for exercise. On the other hand it constituted about five percent of his entire wardrobe. He finally admitted it was a rag which could be sacrificed for the beautiful Chrysler.

Before starting he prayed again. His teacher from second grade and high school, Ms. Sally, would not have been the least bit surprised. He offered the car back to God and committed it to His service. He felt he had never had much to offer before, but he knew if anything happened to the car, it already belonged to God, so it would actually be His loss, not Christopher's. He did not have to stipulate that, of course, he would be the driver since God did not actually drive.

For the next two hours he washed then waxed the car including the door frames. He polished the polish. Then he vacuumed everything over and over, first the trunk which was like a cavern and then the front and back seats. He used his mother's second hand Rainbow vacuum with its water filter. The previous driver, Tiny, the drug smuggling mule for La Coneja, had only used the trunk and the driver's area. Apparently, neither the original owner nor Tiny were smokers. The ash tray was still pristine and the windows were not encrusted with yellow nicotine tar. In some modern cars the plastic puts off a gas which clouds the glass especially in the heat of the desert. There was none of that, either.

Thinking about the original owner brought to mind a remarkable encounter in the middle of his extraordinary yesterday. While Homer, the garage owner, chauffeur, and financier, and his mother were inside the sheriff's pungent office purchasing the car, Christopher met a most unusual man with a very interesting story.

He was sitting on the trunk of an old, faded, powder blue Plymouth Fury parked beside the Chrysler shelling and eating peanuts. Even if he had never opened his mouth except to eat peanuts, he would have been very interesting. The Plymouth was as filthy as the Chrysler except for the section of the trunk being accidentally polished by this deputy sheriff's pants. He was cracking the peanuts and shaking the contents into the palm of his right hand. From there the peanuts were vacuumed into his mouth. Christopher considered what the odds were that the very heavy deputy chose a car beside his to sit on out of all the cars in the very big impound area. The deputy was not fat. He was thick, solid. In fact, in his uniform he resembled a mud brown silo that Christopher had seen near the small town of Clint on his way to Sierra Blanca. The look on the deputy's face said he found life not just fascinating but also very funny.

"You buyin' this car?"

"My mother is buying it for me with the help of the mechanic who brought us here." Christopher did not speak further. He waited. The deputy enjoyed this comfortable silence.

He was savoring this tiny drama and found it profoundly funny. This went on for about ten peanuts.

"The original owner wants to meet you. He lives in an assisted living facility in Van Horn thirty miles further east."

"I can't drive yet. No license."

"Yep. He has an annual physical scheduled in El Paso at William Beaumont Military Hospital next week. I'm driving him. "I'm Joe."

"I'm Christopher. Does he want his car back?"

"No,sir. In fact, he's the one who told the judge to find a worthy buyer and to send him to Homer."

"Why did he do that? Why does he want to talk to me?"

A few more peanuts were temporarily liberated then vacuumed. "He said he thinks it is his assignment." Christopher heard that like a clap of thunder.

"For now, he wants to ask you to garage the car if possible and lock the garage. He wants you not to change the air filter until you have spoken to him. He suggests you not talk about the car, yet."

This very heavy deputy was becoming even more interesting.

"Agreed. Why?"

"His son had a guardianship imposed on him and had him put in an assisted living facility and sold all his possessions including the car. He will tell you he is ok with all that now. He wants the car to go to a worthy person. We are friends, so he sent me to tell you this much. Why he wants you to have this car and why these instructions, you can ask him."

"I will do exactly what he said." Flashing back to Ms. Sally and second grade, he asked, "By the way, can you float?"

"Maybe in the Dead Sea." This abrupt change of topic struck the deputy as odd but very funny. "So, anyway, since your mother is not back yet with your banker, I will tell you one story about this town. The district attorney from El Paso is also in charge of prosecuting felonies in this county and in the next and sends a highly trained assistant district attorney for court once a week in each county before a traveling judge.

"All misdemeanors including all traffic offenses, DWIs, family violence and theft or intentional damage up to $1500 are supposed to be prosecuted by our county attorney. A few years ago the elected county attorney got sideways with the county commissioners and they reduced his salary. He prosecuted less, so they reduced his pay again. He said he could not afford to go to the distant justice courts of this huge county to prosecute the misdemeanors and for several years nobody was prosecuted for misdemeanors.

"One man knew all this and beat his wife repeatedly. Our biggest deputy arrested him, and he was released on bail which he thought meant nothing further was going to happen. The deputy told him if he saw one more mark on the man's wife he was going to take him out in the desert for a 'good thumping.'

"A federal civil rights attorney hired by the wife beater contacted the assistant district attorney and wanted to charge the deputy with official oppression. The assistant district attorney said in every other county in the United States the attorney would have a good case but since there was no legal protection for the wife in this county, the threat of physical violence to protect a third party was allowed. He said he even thought physical violence would be allowed to protect her.

"The next election brought in a new county attorney who prosecuted misdemeanors except against Willie Nelson whose personal bus was stopped at the checkpoint with a Class B amount of marijuana. The county attorney said in the town paper he thought the charge would go away if Willie would just sing Blue Eyes Crying in the Rain.

"Let's go find your mom. I'll show you around a little on the way. This is the oldest adobe courthouse in continued use in Texas. It is two story which is unusual for an adobe building. The jury dormitory is upstairs. This county is so old and so big that when people came for jury duty, they had to come the night before on horseback and stay overnight until the trial was over. The jury in olden times was all men. They were given a deck of cards and a bottle of whiskey and told to stay upstairs.

"Here comes your mom."

"Thank you. I will see you next week."

The man who got out of the back seat of Deputy Joe's black, late model Impala in front of Lupe and Christopher's house did not seem extraordinary in any way. Joe acted as if his conversation with Christopher had been interrupted by only a few seconds and that life was still extremely funny. He began, "So, anyway..." He introduced Christopher to Jim Keeling, a retired owner of a car dealership in Midland. By prearrangement, Joe was to visit Christopher's mom and sample her chile rellenos, Poblano chile peppers covered with an egg batter and stuffed with asadero cheese, and leave the former and current Chrysler owners to visit. It began slowly.

"How was your week?"

"Pretty nice. I worked at Homer's garage three evenings and learned a lot. At school the assistant principal pointed at his eyes with two fingers and then at me to show he is watching me. Everyone else was very nice. How was your week?"

Jim smiled and said, "Nice of you to ask, Christopher. Last year a visiting probate judge granted my son a limited guardianship over me. In this state a guardianship can only extend as far as necessary to protect the person or his property. I can go almost anywhere I want during the day but must return to the facility where I live for my evening medication.

"To answer your question, the probate judge allowed me $1,000 outside the guardianship and any amount I make from that. I have been pretty busy this week on my tablet with the stock market and with various ventures. Most of this week I have not even had time to leave the facility.

"So, now we get to the business at hand, the car. You are very interested, but you are too polite to ask."

What he said was obviously true. There was nothing for Christopher to say, so he just watched Mr. Keeling. He saw a thin, clean shaven man probably in his seventies. What hair he had was nicely trimmed. His clothes were not new, clean but inexpensive. Not dollar store.

"This is all very simple. The last money I made before my son had me declared partly incompetent I put in the Chrysler where the huge air filter normally goes. When Junior had me declared partly incompetent and sold my car to the disreputable bar owner, I could do nothing.

"When it was confiscated from Tiny as the instrument of a crime and I heard it was getting poor gas mileage, I was very pleased and called my favorite justice of the peace in Clint to find a decent person to buy it. I have no need for the car and no right to its contents. My son has looked very hard for the money but knows very little about cars. Since he sold the car he is not entitled to its contents. His search has brought me more enjoyment than anything else I can remember. Everything is original except the windshield which I replaced to make it stronger. You will probably never notice it.

"I have made more money again than I stored in this car and can only eat three meals a day, so you are welcome to it. If you trust me, Joe can give you a receipt for the contents of the air filter and wire it to your mother's account within two days. It will be held in trust for you until then. There are tax issues and my accountant will call on you and your mother next week. Also, if you are interested, I will see you from time to time and tell you about things I think are promising investments. Bear in mind I am under a guardianship.

"It will be safer if you do not draw attention to yourself or the car for now. You might just want to pay for the car slowly with your paycheck as planned. The air filter is getting harder to find so we brought one with us. Maybe we could all go to the garage now and try it out."

••••••

Christopher did not take his car to school even when he had gotten his license, inspection, registration, and insurance. His mother worked nearby and did not drive and his school and their church were both very close, also. The car did get much better gas mileage after the obstruction in the air filter was removed.

Homer's garage had a contract with the county to service the sheriff's cars from the valley substation. Part of Christopher's job was to change the oil in them and in that way he interacted with many of the deputies. He was always courteous and sincere and slowly the deputies replaced the impression of him that they had been given by his assistant principal. They recalled he was the one who had respectfully and formally bowed to the SWAT team. Homer told the deputies that he had given Christopher driving lessons for his license and was slowly financing the car bought for him at the auction.

As promised, the accountant of Mr. Keeling had worked with Christopher and his mother. He helped them with the signature cards at the bank to place the "air filter money" into an account in both their names. He helped prepare Christopher's first tax return.

Christopher was not sure what God wanted him to do with the money. He considered it an assignment, but this would take even more prayer than the car. The old priest at his parish said to talk to God. Then he added, "When you talk to Him, it would be good to let Him do some of the talking."

The old man reminded him of their favorite sermon. "When you stand before the Eternal Tribunal, the Lord will not ask how many servants you had or how many cars. 'What did you do for your eternal reward?' "

Christopher thought about that often. He began to withdraw money every month for his mother for utilities and for food and repairs. She had inherited the adobe house from her parents, and slowly began to use the money to catch up on long deferred maintenance including the roof and re-stuccoing the exterior. None of these expenditures even put a dent in the amount that was in the bank.

Along with his senior classmates, he had heard that the entire class might not graduate. Not, Bobby, not Adam or his sister, Stephanie. Not even Carmine who had scholarships waiting for him.

He wanted to be certified as a mechanic, but being a dropout or a "kickout" would slow that plan down. He went to his pecan tree customer, the semi-retired attorney across the street from the school, to ask his advice.

The attorney told him that there was to be a court in his class that former Judge Howell taught the following week and not to miss school. Christopher might be asked to testify regarding the assistant principal's false accusations or Christopher might be allowed to sign an affidavit of all the facts and be excused as a witness.The attorney would be there as an observer. As it turned out he would be there as attorney for both Christopher and Adam.

BOBBY, GUISEPPE, AND JEAN PATRICE

He was delusional and thought the staff was trying to kill him. He had broken a mirror, a vase, a lamp, and a heavy oak chair in less than ten minutes and was ready to do battle with all of them, except Jean Patrice.The exhausted child finally sat on the brown tiled floor of the conference room he had done his best to destroy. The half dozen staff members kept their distance and understood more clearly why children rarely attended these staffings. Mucous was running freely down his lips and chin and onto his little bare chest. His now buttonless shirt had been torn open earlier in his thrashing with the police who had brought him here very carefully. He had new scrapes and old scars all over his arms and chest. He glared at everyone and cursed them richly and guaranteed them that they could not kill him. Jean Patrice slipped out of the room unnoticed and returned with a warm washcloth and sat on the floor beside him. The staff watched mesmerized as this formidable fifty pound child allowed the administrator to dry his eyes and wipe clean his face and his chest.

The warm moisture of the cloth caused him to relax a little and stop crying. She produced a starched, ironed handkerchief from the sleeve of her habit and shook it open. "Blow your nose, buddy."

He had not slept for three full days, and had come under police escort straight here from the crackhouse where his mother and father had been arrested. He was calmer but not sleepy.

The staff was fascinated as they watched this skinny five year old make maximum, noisy use of the handkerchief and hand it back to the administrator. She was simply not part of his delusion. This was the first time he had met her and she was now a lifelong friend. She tucked away the handkerchief and washcloth nonchalantly. Without all the mucous, his breathing was growing more steady. The room was silent like in a play when the audience is preparing itself for the next scene. She waited a little longer. "I want you to go with Steven to the kitchen. He will feed you. When you are ready, I will see you in my office."

Steven was on the side of Jean Patrice and was, therefore, in the child's mind, not one of the killers. He was a giant to the five year old, taller than the administrator, even taller than his father. To the boy he looked like a six-story building. More importantly for the moment, he was a cook. After a hamburger and french fries followed by cherry pie, without being asked, Bobby told him a fractured version of his last day and a half. The police had raided a crackhouse in the projects, his mother was arrested and in the hospital. His father was arrested for disturbing the peace, some of the officers were dead. They had blood all over them. His mother's relatively coherent ramblings to the officers accurately included that the blood on their uniforms came from a large gash on the father's head courtesy of the crack dealer and was sustained before the police arrived. There were no fatalities, and no officers were injured. According to the mother, the father had "gone all God on her and quit meth and was only there to rescue the child."

Reality was illusive even in the kitchen. Bobby was tortured by many of his intermittent alternate realities. The people in the picture on the wall above the long prep table were laughing at him, whispering that the staff was still going to kill him when Steven wasn't there. A layman would call his sudden mood shifts mercurial; doctors called them labile. Jean Patrice knew that the drug induced psychosis was caused just by breathing the horrible air in his former residence and would hopefully wear off after several months. His insomnia and nightmares when he did sleep and episodes of non-reality and extreme paranoia would also subside. Then he would just be terribly disturbed and for all practical purposes an orphan. Meanwhile he had not slept in several days and the leather couch in Jean Patrice's office was very comfortable. He was safe and full and drowsy. Steven sat, silent, and did not leave until the boy was asleep.

When Bobby awoke hours later he saw Jean Patrice at her desk computer entering notes regarding his admission. Weeks ago, his father had requested that Bobby be allowed to live at the center and that the center have temporary conservatorship over him. The family law judge agreed, but Bobby was only located very early today.

His mother had signed a relinquishment of her parental rights and the family law court accepted her relinquishment affidavit but oddly did not terminate her rights. The judge listened to the father and then made two rulings which surprised almost everyone. The father was granted joint managing conservatorship with the center. The center would retain superior right of possession and superior right to determine where the child would live. The father would have liberal visitation upon continued clean drug tests and compliance with prescribed medication. The court's order said that the father and son would have a lifetime relationship and the judge saw no reason to damage it by terminating the father's parental rights. The judge told the mother that, although he was very old, he hoped to review her relinquishment of parental rights at the end of two years and he would either finalize it or allow her to withdraw it.

Some of the children at the center attended the public grade school or the public high school on the other side of the center's playing fields. Until he made a great deal of progress, Bobby would attend the on-campus school which was paid for by the same school district and staffed partly by the district and supplemented by the center's staff. Jean Patrice was the principal of this school. In place of a mascot the school's symbol was a volcano.The schools and center were separated only by the track and field grounds and the soccer field. The center owned the fields and was good about sharing.

In his fourth month at the center Bobby was beginning individual counseling with a therapist who really did not like him. It probably did not help that Bobby who could not even read yet wore a donated t-shirt with large print: Reality is Overrated.The therapist's dislike for Bobby did not weaken the strategies the therapist was teaching. Bobby was taught to first tell a story and then retell it choosing which parts were real and which imaginary. Some of Bobby's stories were real but very difficult to believe.

When Jean Patrice was with him and he was having delusions, she would use an old Groucho Marx line, "Who are you going to believe, me or your eyes?"

Today Bobby was fifteen minutes late for his after-school session and the therapist was outside the office door of the administrator on the second floor complaining bitterly. Jean Patrice stood at her window and watched a very interesting drama playing out on the oval track below. She had just seen Bobby throw his backpack to the side and begin running in the lane next to a girl whom Jean Patrice recognized as a student of the public high school. She was on the school's varsity track team and apparently did not mind Bobby running beside her. The girl did not appear to have slowed her pace to accommodate him. They had completed one full lap together when Jean Patrice closed the drapes and turned her attention to the angry therapist who was ready to talk or explode.

"What I am about to say will make you very angry, but I feel I should say it anyway. This child is being coddled and I actually think it is at your direction. He comes from a criminal family and needs to be taught that his parents are experiencing the consequences of their crimes. I think he should be taught to be very angry with them and to verbalize his anger toward them."

"Active listening" dictates that the listener exactly match the level of emotion of the speaker in nearly, but not, the same words.

The therapist was still standing in the doorway of the office when she said to him, "You feel so strongly about what you are saying that you have to confront me even though it will make me very angry. You feel I am spoiling Bobby by not forcing him to confront his parents about how they have damaged him."

Active listening works even on people who know how it works. Most people cannot resist being heard. Paraphrasing prevents people from feeling they are being mimicked.

The therapist took a few steps into the office and said in a barely more conciliatory tone, "But he also needs to be pushed further physically to maximize his anti-psychotic medications and enable him to sleep better."

"You feel he needs very strong exercise in conjunction with his prescriptions to reduce psychotic episodes and help him sleep. He could be told to run with the girl's varsity track team after school every day. We could convert one of his therapy sessions to a physical therapy session. I will see to that. In fact, consider it done. Thanks."

"I actually thought we were going to have a huge confrontation and that I would then submit my resignation."

"You were expecting a huge clash and you would then announce that you were leaving. We haven't spoken about either one of those things. Next week at this same time Bobby will be in track therapy and we can talk. I am very glad you came to see me. Thank you."

⎯⎯⎯⎯⎯ ✦✦✦✦✦ ⎯⎯⎯⎯⎯

He locked the door of his apartment above the triple garage. This campus had been his home for twelve years. His episodes of paranoia and illusion very slowly left him and he entered the campus school. After ten years he finally entered the public high school where he was as stable as most of his senior class. He thought of his good friends, Christopher, Adam, Stephanie, and their fearless leader, Carmine. And Giuseppe. He would eat dinner at a restaurant where Giuseppe was the waiter. That made him smile.

All of the current residents at the center were younger than Bobby. The average stay was two years, not twelve. He hopes to graduate from high school in two months and be the first resident to take advantage of state paid college tuition if he registers by the time he turns twenty-one.

Bobby knew this Friday night was going to be a little difficult but good. He was walking to the restaurant of a schoolmate one year behind him where he would have dinner with his father who wanted to voluntarily enter a brief rehab program. It was something like a booster shot. Under his arm he carried a gift for the schoolmate who would be their waiter. Later he would be introduced to a detective that Jean Patrice wanted him to meet.

Recently a classmate and friend, Christopher, aptly named "the disciple," had suggested he learn to count his blessings. As he walked the four blocks from his residential treatment center through the historic district to meet his dad, that thought occurred to him. He did not know much about God, but still said he was grateful to be alive, to be meeting his dad who was improving, to be free of hallucinations. Thinking God might have a sense of humor, he said, "I think I am not hallucinating any more, and thank You for Sister Patrice, my counselor."

He thought with a smile about this evening's waiter whose school nickname was "Juice," short for Giuseppe, a small well-liked junior. His gray eyes were set in a face that was pleasant, good- natured, humorous but not comical. Bobby thought the gifts he was carrying would help.

Juice's grades were, fortunately, above average. Decent grades were his mom's requirement for keeping his part time job in her restaurant after school and on weekends. A severe speech impediment prevented him from speaking, but he had done his best to turn it to his advantage.

Most of his customers had been waited on by his mother and his grandparents for years and now enjoyed being waited on by Giuseppe. He was very attentive to them. He remembered where they wanted to sit, their favorite dishes right down to the salad dressing, and their choice of wine. When they would order white wine his grandmother used to say, "Thanks, you know the red stains my feet." Always amusing. He could not say that but could dramatically stare at his feet and nod appreciation for white or show concern when they ordered red. Still amusing.

His customers recommended the restaurant and Giuseppe to their family and friends. "Great food, great service but remember, the waiter doesn't speak. You will know who he is, he has a pumpkin colored afro."

Tonight the solicitous, young waiter with his Italian afro kept an eye on Bobby, who was his final customer and a senior at Giuseppe's school, while replacing a white, starched tablecloth where a family with children had eaten earlier. The parents left an extra large tip because they said the tablecloth now looked like a Jackson Pollack painting.

There was no evidence of the antipasto salad or the eggplant parmesan cooked by his mother and served to Bobby earlier. The bowl and plate had been mopped clean with some of the buttery garlic bread which came with the meal. The waiter saw the clean bowl and plate and with a raised eyebrow and surprised look indicated he was impressed. Across the table an order of baked lasagna sat, beautiful but no longer hot. The carafe of red wine was also untouched. The waiter looked at the food and then at his customer as if pained but that he understood.

Bobby, had deeper thoughts than his father's missed meal but appreciated that Giuseppe silently sympathized. His own meal was over, but his concentration was focused across the table, through the large window overlooking the parking lot, where the his father was talking quietly with five police officers. Everyone was being pleasant.

Bobby was pleased to see that two of the officers were from crisis intervention and that they knew his father. They were trained to be non-confrontational. It also helped that it was his father, sensing a meltdown, who had called the hotline for help. Two of the officers were backup because of the father's size and prior history of volatility and the last officer just happened to be in the neighborhood and knew exactly where the restaurant was.

A family law judge had granted joint managing conservatorship of Bobby to his father and to the center where he had lived for the past twelve years. His counselor, whom Bobby had mentioned to God earlier, lived across campus and had helped him shorten his name from "psycho Bobby" to "just Bobby" in that time. She had been his principal also until he transferred from the Center's high school to the public high school in the next block. He would be emancipated in a few months. His progress in therapy now allowed visits with his dad and near autonomy in making decisions.

The father walked with one of the intervention officers to an unmarked unit and got into the front seat. He would enter a rehab facility voluntarily for a "tune up", a readjustment of his medications. That might take up to a week. He had emptied his pockets on the table and asked Bobby to hold his wallet and keys to his car and shop for a while.

Meanwhile Bobby turned to his waiter and made a writing motion in the air for the check. Giuseppe made a production of searching his pockets and apron for a pencil then withdrew one from his storage compartment, his hair. He crossed off the untouched wine and handed the bill to Bobby. He then boxed the father's lasagna, salad, and all the remaining garlic bread to go. Bobby took the money from his father's wallet and placed it on the table to cover two meals and an appropriate tip. Giuseppe nodded in appreciation and then saw that Bobby was leaving a box on the table, the size of a shoe box. Giuseppe pointed at the box so that Bobby would not forget it, but Bobby pointed at Giuseppe to indicate it was for him and said that he should open it.

Bobby's father was a tailor. Bobby had made the hand puppet in his shop— a nearly perfect replica of Giuseppe with perfect teeth, the signature pumpkin colored afro, the red apron, even a tiny pencil protruding from the hair. Giuseppe beamed a great smile and nodded to Bobby, not sure yet what it meant, but Bobby knew. There was also a disc in the box showing a comedian.

Bobby had seen Albert Brooks on a late night Johnny Carson rerun. He was a ventriloquist with a speak and spell dummy wearing a cheap, blonde wig with pigtails.

"Say 'Hi' to Johnny."

He pulled the string on the speak and spell.

"A."

Bobby was walking in the direction of the Center and slowed when he came to a house with a wraparound porch where his principal and Jean Patrice were sitting in rockers. He nodded to the principal and nodded and smiled to Jean Patrice. He noticed a young couple approaching the house from the opposite direction on the sidewalk. Mr. Skousin invited everyone up onto the porch and Jean Patrice said, "This is Detective David Lambchild, Bobby, walking toward us, but I do not know this young lady yet."

Bobby put his carryout from the restaurant in his left hand and extended his right. "Just Bobby."

"My friends call me David David. Glad to meet you. This is Jillian Walsh. I have asked her to marry me and she is considering it."

Bobby asked her, "Your father is the warden?"

She answered, "Yes," and seemed to enjoy the look of surprise on everyone's face and the shock on David's face. Recovering slightly, David explained that he had been requested to appear in Judge David Howell's class as a witness. I will see you there next week.

———— ‹‹‹‹›››› ————

The disc of the ventriloquist Albert Brooks was all it took. Bobby started greeting Juice at school loudly with just that single syllable—A.

Then it was Giuseppe's turn. He saw an old Pink Panther movie where the Chinese butler was required to sneak up on the inspector and attack him to keep him alert. It took a week of practice to make the 'A' sound. He had to wear the hand puppet for confidence, but he was now ready and only waiting for the opportune time. Or inopportune time. Surprise became an essential element of the game.

A week after Bobby's interrupted meal, the principal stood in the center of the intersection of the school's two main hallways. Streams of students went around him and Bobby, almost everyone hustling to their third period classes.

The principal's back was to Juice as he simply and silently observed Bobby. His arms were folded, as always, as he nodded his head up and down, as always. Two separate reports had come to the principal that

Giuseppe was being bullied, possibly by Bobby. One of the reports came from the assistant principal and was, therefore, suspect.

The principal had a reputation for being very tough and very fair. Many situations were resolved that never even reached him just because everyone knew what should happen and what would happen. "Mr. Skousin isn't going to like this" could be said by students or teachers to remind the opposition of what would happen on appeal. Mr. Skousin had been a teacher at Bobby's grade school at the center and then was assigned to this high school at the same time that Bobby transferred to the school. The principal was just back after a two month absence for surgery and recovery.

Meanwhile, Giuseppe removed the hand puppet from his back pack long enough to say "A" in a loud voice and then replace the puppet. The principal turned to see the source of the noise and saw Giuseppe in a crowd. The principal was silent and thoughtful, nodding his head as he considered what was going on. Giuseppe was the picture of innocence. He withdrew the sock puppet again and said to the principal, "A" and and then raised his chin toward Bobby to indicate he had just delivered a challenge. Finally, the principal turned back to Bobby still nodding his head and waiting.

"I am teaching him to talk. He needs a puppet for confidence. And he is waiting for a response." It was almost a plea for permission. Then to Juice, "A." Then to the principal, "I taught him one other thing to say in his chemistry class. I will get to my third period English class now." The principal continued to nod his head with his arms folded. Problem solved without a word spoken.

That afternoon notes were delivered to Giuseppe and Bobby and one to the chemistry teacher.

"The bearer of this note, Mr. Giuseppe Serafino, has my permission to use his service puppet to speak at any time." Signed Mr. Larry Skousin.

"Mr. Stone, Giuseppe Serafino may speak briefly and unexpectedly in your chemistry class. I hope you will encourage his beginning speech. Thank you." Larry Skousin.

"The bearer of this note, Mr. Bobby O'Mara, has my permission to speak briefly to Mr. Giuseppe Serafino at any time." Signed Mr. Larry Skousin.

The notes were very timely. Especially in chemistry. "Giuseppe, can you tell the class the symbol for gold?" It was an unwritten rule that no one called on Giuseppe to recite. Giuseppe's very loud response sounded like, "Hey, you," directed to Mr. Stone. The teacher turned to his class and said, "Got it? Au. Thank you, Giuseppe."

+ + ♦ ♦ ♦ + +

Meanwhile, the class of retired Judge David Howell was preparing to receive a legal delegation.

THE SUBSTITUTE TEACHER

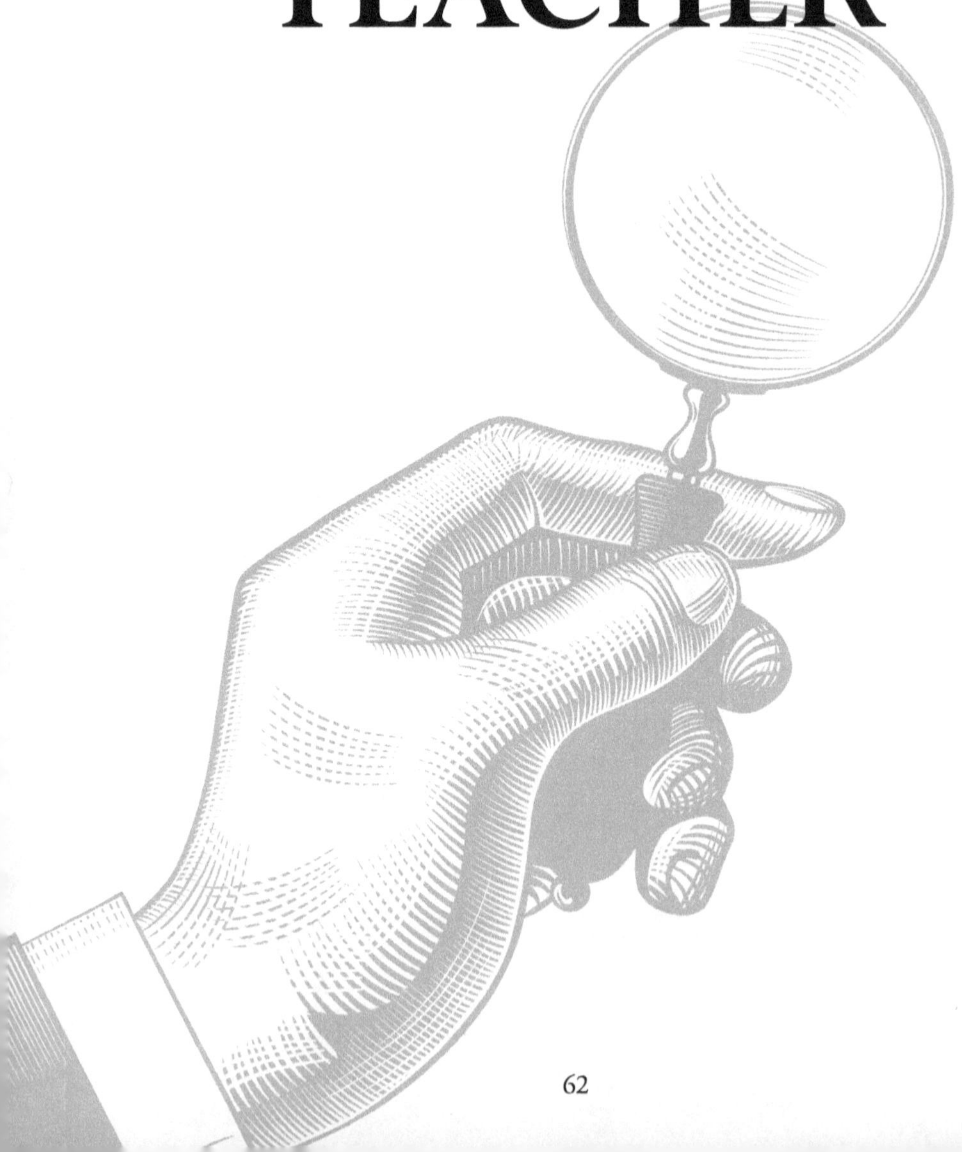

For six months following his retirement, he had been busier than at any time he could remember, although, admittedly, his memory was one of the reasons he had retired.

Among many other projects, he had rebuilt the double hung window in his living room, so that it now opened for the first time in thirty years. The cross breeze was welcome. He would open and close it just to admire the results of his long unused carpentry skills. His lifelong friend, David Lee, a carpenter who specialized in furniture restoration during his career, helped him and while they worked they remembered the Lee's personal restoration more than twenty years before.

Following the death of their teen age daughter, the Lees were depressed and unconsolable. A year after their loss a delegation from Mount Shiloh Church asked to meet with them at their house with a shocking proposal. For just over five years the church community had raised a child abandoned on the park bench just outside the church one Sunday morning as services began. Their singing had awakened the baby whose loud crying announced his arrival and who was immediately christened "Lambchild." He was clothed, and fed, and loved the same as every child in the congregation. He lived at all the houses and everyone was family. At the age of five, Lambchild witnessed the late night abduction of a young lady and tried to stop it. The abductor broke Lambchild's arm, kicked him in the face, and threatened to kill him following church services in front of most of the congregation.

The delegation from the church asked to Lees to adopt this child for his protection and because they could not legally register him for school.

The adoption took place in the court of the Honorable John Howell (now retired) and was memorable. The judge tried to persuade Mrs. Lee that the child should have the Lee's last name, but she prevailed. He tried to persuade Mr. Lee that the child should not have the same first and middle name. The father prevailed. The Lees listed his birthplace as Mount Shiloh Church (park bench).

The Judge asked the newly named David David Lambchild on what day he was born and the child said, "On the very first day."

The judge had watched David David progress through school and through the police academy. When his background check was run for his substitute teaching certificate, there were no hits but the now retired judge thought it was an interesting co-incidence that David David had been assigned to run the judge's name for any criminal history.

Today David Howell invited David Lee and David David Lambchild to enjoy coffee and a cross breeze in his living room and to discuss the future.

His friends from downtown told him, "It's not like when you taught forty years ago. Kids are different today. You're old school. You will be miserable, possibly even in danger. Call us." He promised to call on them for help. Although their offers were made humorously, they were sincere and, as it turned out, very fortunate.

He knew he lacked the immense energy of his youth, his computer skills were weak and his memory was intermittently very good or very bad. He was banking on the advice he had received from his first principal, a legend, "If you like your students, they will like you no matter how tough you are. If you don't like them, they will know it and will make your life miserable."

Fortunately, the "formerly honorable" Judge John Howell as his friends called him liked everyone and looked forward to working with young people who could still make good decisions about their futures. He was assigned to the high school for the last two months of the school year. Specifically, he was assigned to a senior class whose teacher was gravely ill through no fault of the class. He would teach English, History and Civics which he was actually licensed to teach with a lifetime teaching certificate, but he had to take all day Math and English tests to refresh his license. So much for lifetime. He was told by the assistant principal that this class had a particularly difficult reputation. This same assistant principal, Mr. Rebele, claimed, with no evidence, that this class had contributed to the teacher's illness and two month leave of absence, the last two months of the school year.

The principal of the school, Mr. Skousin, also believed that students knew if you liked or disliked them. He took Judge Howell all over the campus the first day and proudly introduced him to coaches, classroom teachers, janitors, students, and cooks. His reputation permeated the school— tough but fair.

The only slightly negative note during the tour occurred when the assistant principal interjected himself during the introduction by Mr. Skousin to another history teacher. Uninvited, Mr. Rebele suggested that Mrs. Bissel's disciplinary style was one Judge Howell would not want to adopt. During this brazen insult, Mr. Skousin folded his arms and began to nod his head up and down, not at all in agreement with the vicious assistant principal's assessment, but to control his own temper. "Mrs. Bissel's love and knowledge of history is astounding. It would not surprise me if some of her students become history teachers."

David Howell had dealt with good people and with bad. He was ready for any class. He was ready for Mr. Rebele, too.

As he entered the classroom for the first time, he got the impression that a class huddle had just ended and had apparently gone well.

Extraordinary classes sometimes have extraordinary leaders. Enter one Carmine Shields, showman, comedian, leader and spokesperson for what would prove to be a truly extraordinary class of students. Carmine raised his hand as the judge was putting his briefcase on his desk. He had wanted to set the tone himself but would field one question first. "Yes"?

"Once a judge always a judge and so, with your permission, that is how we will address you. We have heard of you. On behalf of this class, judge, I have been designated to welcome you to our school and to this class. We want to make your time with us productive and entertaining — even memorable. We are trying to graduate and cannot let the unfortunate loss of our regular teacher mean loss of credits. We are a good class and we need to graduate. My name is Carmine. We will wear these name tags until you know us."

"Thank you, Carmine." He surveyed the class to see if the spokesperson accurately represented the sentiment of the class and saw Carmine's message reflected in the earnest faces of the young men and women before him. He wondered how Carmine was designated the spokesperson. Some attorneys who had appeared before him could have learned a few things about advocacy from Carmine. He wanted to know how a good class acquired a bad reputation. This idea would help him set the tone and shape his relationship with this class.

"Honesty is not overrated. It is cherished; its value is appreciated. In our language we actually announce when we are going to use it. 'To tell you the truth.', 'Let me be honest with you.'. 'Honestly.' Even 'Sincerely yours' at the end of a letter means without wax, that is to say, 'Between us we do not need wax and a seal to show what I have written you is trustworthy.'

"Speaking of telling the truth, I have very early signs of dementia, but I will make it to your graduation two months from now. In court a lawyer can say, 'As the court is well aware' and proceed to respectfully remind or tell the court what it already knows or should know. Here you could say, 'You may remember.' and I will always consider that respectful. Please do not abuse that privilege by trying to remind me of something false.

"There are those who feel the truth is like a sharp knife that should not be dulled by constant use. I do not like that. I propose to you that your word is everything. No truth, no you.

"I have made several decisions in the few minutes since I met you. In one month I want a mock trial in the form of a court of inquiry in this room to last one hour. I want to know why this class is disliked and threatened with not graduating. Several members of the judiciary and of the county bar association have offered to help me as if I need protection from you. Having met you, I believe it is this class that needs protection. I may call on my old friends to assist you. If you are assigned to be a prosecutor, you will have a mentor, but be ready to defend. The same goes for the defense. Be ready to change sides. That way you will know both sides of the argument. This court will not have power to subpoena outside witnesses as it would if a sitting judge were to conduct the court.

"So far, I know of false charges of gang membership and drug charges and theft of a firearm against one of you and a false murder accusation against another one of you. A young detective whose adoption I handled in my court twenty years ago has been assigned to investigate all criminal charges against members of this class. Do not be offended. He also had to check my background before I could become your teacher.

"At the end of this hour, I want you to know how many credits you have, I want you to write down what you plan on becoming, and I want you to realistically determine when your parents want you to move out of the house. I hear you laughing lightly, but that is part of your life plan and theirs. Your vocation or calling or career is only a dream until you write it down. Then it's a plan. Write your plan down, too."

A young man raised his hand. "I want you to know who I am. My name is Adam. I will wear an extra large name tag until you remember me. If I am the cause of this class maybe not graduating, I want to take that blame alone."

The next day, following Adam's example, every student in his senior class wore an oversized name tag and agreed to remove it only when the judge consistently remembered the name on it.

Four times in the next two weeks young Mr. Carmine Shields raised his hand. In history class he asked, "Did Franz list?" and David Howell like a straight man in a comedy duo explained who Franz Liszt was and played a recording of Liebestraum and finished by saying that he was not aware of any leanings of Mr. Liszt, political or physical.

During a discussion on evolution in class the next week, Carmine asked if Dr. Louis Leakey's theories still held water. Very funny. The students paid attention just to see what was going to happen.

English class was not safe either. "Did William Faulkner really write The Bear? Why would anyone write to a bear?"

"Was Aesop fable-minded?"

The students enjoyed this immensely, but their substitute finally play acted that he was really confused. "Mr. Shields, may I see you in my chambers or, rather, sorry, in the hallway?"

In the hallway the former judge asked, as if in some sort of fugue, "So, why did you ask to see me? Why did you call me out here?"

"Wow, this is like you're non campus mentis. I was just trying to make things interesting, judge. Are you ok?"

The assistant principal of the school came by and interrupted, "Are you having trouble controlling your class? This troublemaker? We have substitutes for substitutes, you know."

Whatever trance David Howell was in, or pretended to be in, vanished. "Let's talk a little further down the hall." It was not a request. When they were out of hearing range of young Mr. Carmine Shields, David said, "The only reason your sister's DWI did not proceed in my court downtown was that the arresting officer's daughter is a senior at this school in my class and he wants her to graduate without any complications. You may apologize to Mr. Shield and then go away."

The forced apology was quickly offered and accepted. The assistant principal went away and David Howell said, "Mr. Shields, would you teach the rest of this class? A lesson plan that is clear and interesting is on the desk. It has vocabulary words, stories and even room for humor. I'll sit in the back, mostly."

Years later when asked why he became a law professor, he would smile and remember a substitute teacher and say, "You might say I was called."

Judge Howell was watching for a chance to teach students how to change a problem into an opportunity. A student announced one day that he had forgotten to bring an assignment that was due. "Class, this is a great opportunity. Isaac , would you please sit in my chair at my desk. I promise you will not be embarrassed because you may choose your attorney."

"I choose Bobby."

"Thank you for your confidence, Isaac. Your honor, class. In the cosmic order of things this is not a great offense. If Isaac can help this class with memory aids, he will have corrected his small mistake twenty-five times. That is the number of students in this class." After a short consultation with his "client," he continued. "Every person in this class should have a weekly planner or calendar, on paper or on the phone. Each of us should have a small appointment book with us almost always. Finally, if we want to absolutely remember to take something to school, for example, we should put it in front of the front door so we cannot escape without it. It is harder if you have little brothers or sisters or a pet that moves things."

"Thank you, Bobby, Isaac. You have corrected the problem twenty-six times since that helps me too. You can also send yourself a message on your phone."

One week before the court of inquiry, the assistant principal entered the classroom of David Howell, uninvited. He deliberately addressed him as Mr. Howell to indicate his respect for him and for his judicial reputation was non-existent.

"Mr. Howell, there are rumors that this class is out of control. I am on the verge of suspending the entire class which will give them failing grades for non-attendance and prevent their graduation in under one month. I have come to see for myself if you have the ability to control this class."

"Would you prefer that I speak to you in the hallway?"

"No, right here."

"Good. welcome to my civics class. Three things:

"First, if you ever come into this class room again uninvited or remain here after I finish talking to you right now and disrupt my class, I will file a sworn Class C complaint and testify against you for disruption of class. As you know, the legislature has eliminated that offense for students who are rightly in the class, but invading adults are not exempt, maximum fine $500.00.

Second, tomorrow you will be served with a subpoena to testify under oath at what is now a lawfully constituted court of inquiry to be conducted in this room by a duly elected district judge next week. Dodging the subpoena is a crime, failing to attend is a crime, perjury is a crime.

Third, in the event there is enough evidence following the court of inquiry, you may be named in a federal lawsuit brought on behalf of this class for violation of federal civil rights for interfering with or preventing this class's education.

In regard to an earlier threat you made regarding this class not graduating, if you are suggesting changing a student's grade, directly or indirectly, to accomplish that unworthy goal, it is a criminal violation of the state's education code for anyone other than the teacher to change a student's grade and that violation is prosecutable under state law and punishable also by a fine for each grade changed.

"Class, since I first spoke about a court of inquiry, there have been developments. Judge Villa is a sitting district judge and he will conduct the court next week. Each of you that have a role will have a mentor attorney. Bobby, you will have an assistant federal prosecutor to assist you as your mentor. You will also have an attorney ad litem, assigned to protect your legal rights. Christopher, the man who lives across the street from the school has volunteered to act as your attorney. He has offered to represent Adam as well.

"Mr. Rebele, I see that Judge Villa has subpoenaed you. You will be entitled to an attorney."

"I might not be available for this little classroom exercise."

No one, including the speaker, could have predicted how true that statement would be or that it would include an injury with a lunchbox or an attempt on his life. "I suspect this young man will not be available, either." He pointed at Adam who did not know that the assistant principal had persuaded a slightly gullible district judge to inexplicably raise the personal recognizance bond on Adam's drug charge to $30,000.00.

He was in compliance with his probation since his last visit to the judge, but that was not satisfactory to the assistant principal.

The very second class was over, Christopher asked Adam to call Christopher's attorney and then asked Adam if he would allow Christopher to speak privately to him using Adam's phone. Adam was amused because he had to show Christopher how to use a cell phone. After the brief call, the disciple asked Adam to trust him and to take a ride with him and to bring his sister.

He had parked the immaculate Chrysler across from the school. Stephanie and Adam were in the cavernous back seat and Adam got out to open the door for Mr. Baumgardner, Christopher's customer and attorney.

Their first stop was the bank where Christopher and the attorney did business. Christopher, now legally an adult and now co-signer on the "air filter" account signed a withdrawal slip and gave the proceeds to Mr. Baumgardner who deposited the proceeds into a trust account and then signed a simple affidavit showing he now had $30,000 unencumbered money in his client trust account and that he was pledging it as an attorney's bond for his recently acquired client, Adam Bohanan.

Their second stop was the sheriff's office where Mr. Baumgardner presented his attorney bond. Attached to the affidavit was the bank receipt for the deposit of the same amount of money. At the request of Mr. Baumgardner, the sheriff allowed Adam to go through the expedited satellite booking which was done away from the jail and took about fifteen minutes and which eliminated the need to be booked into the jail and then released, a process that would have taken several hours and would have prevented Adam from attending class in the afternoon.

This process also allowed the source of the money beyond Mr. Baumgardner to remain undisclosed. In confidence, Christopher had told his attorney all about Mr. Jim Keeling, the retired car dealer and original owner of the car. The attorney told him his money was safe as long as Adam appeared when required. Adam was embarrassed and said, "How could anyone pick up that number of cans? Thank you."

The next day David Howell was confronted by the assistant principal in the office who smugly announced that Adam would not be out of jail in time for the court of inquiry. "A thirty thousand dollar bond won't be easy to raise." David Howell knew nothing about the raised bond or the actions of Mr. Baumgardner for his other client. The judge did know that Stefanie and Adam were sitting in his classroom and had asked to speak to him with Christopher and Carmine present.

Carmine was the spokesperson. "Judge, we know we are not allowed to speak to Judge Villa about the information that will be covered in the court of inquiry. On the other hand some of this class are close to not passing and need to study for our finals. We cannot use up too much of that study time on the court of inquiry. We have spoken with the attorneys assigned, and we want to make offers of evidence to eliminate or reduce witness testimony. You said originally that the Court would last one hour and be over. Even though events have mushroomed, we can stick with that schedule.

"We have had the help of the attorneys assigned to us and we can submit an affidavit by Detective Lambchild to prove that no one killed Ms. Sanchez, the English teacher. Adam will submit his affidavit stating that he is out on an attorney's bond and expects to graduate with the class. Christopher's affidavit will tell of his false arrest for gang membership and will relate the SWAT incident caused by Mr. Rebele's false accusations.The main witness would be Mr. Rebele to actually testify why he is trying to prevent our graduation. We should be done in one hour as you originally planned. Alice will address the attempted murder."

Even an assault and an attempted murder spree would not extend the court beyond one hour.

THE REBELES AND MR. STACK

The adoption agency's small staff did not like her and she did not care. She was especially not liked by the counselor for the pre-adolescent potential adoptees who was presently glaring at her. The counselor was looking at a woman in her mid thirties with straight, dark hair of medium length, a style once called Prince Valiant or page boy which the counselor thought had gone out of style more than fifty years ago, except for the Beatles.

The counselor thought that her heavy clod shoes and dark war refugee ensemble could not have looked any worse and this uncharacteristic, uncharitable observation told her how really furious she was. For the hundredth time the counselor missed the flair and kindness and wisdom of the former administrator, her friend, whom she would visit at the stroke rehab center this evening. In her mind she began drafting her resignation letter.

This administrator was dogmatic and sure of herself, the exact opposite of her predecessor who liked and listened to her staff. Ms. Rebele and her brother had taken over an agency when the prior owner and administrator had a massive, paralyzing stroke. This administrator simply announced her short conclusions repeatedly and allowed no staff input.

Today's decision regarding Danny's immediate adoption hit the counselor like a bolt of lightening from a clear, blue sky. Mary Clark could deal with sarcasm, rage, deceit, and a modicum of violence in her small clients and often did to further a child's therapy goals and to smooth an appropriate adoption placement.

This was different. She knew from witnessing two months of horrible, unilateral decision making that the director's mind was made up and there would be no appeal. For Danny's sake, she would try although she suspected a profitable financial arrangement had already been made.

"Please, Ms. Rebele. Danny needs therapy before he is adopted. He is not stable."

"Every child is adoptable. Every child is adoptable."

"Please. Danny started classes in the third grade today and walked three blocks to get there. In that short walk he saw or thought he saw a boy fall into a swimming pool and saw or thought he saw a crossing guard stabbed multiple times. I worked with him this afternoon to help him separate facts from fantasy."

"Every child is adoptable, even ones with imagination. This adoptive parent says he wants a challenge and has hired a couple and some others to help train him. Mr. Rebele, my brother, agrees. This matter is settled."

During the years since, the adoptive father, a Mr. Stack, saw the child annually to receive a report from the couple he had hired regarding Danny's home training and schooling. At the same time he obtained a report from others regarding Danny's special training including martial arts and marksmanship. This year's reports were determinative.

Mr. Stack was in reality a very evil man. He was also practical. His plan to train Danny as an assassin was not working out. True, Danny was an excellent marksman and had other skills that might have aided him in that profession, but a grip on reality was a necessity to acquire and maintain a particular target and to plan and execute a killing was not in the gentle nature of Danny who liked everyone.

Mr. Stack perused the most recent reports from the boy's caregivers and from his "special trainers." He decided to eliminate his mistake himself to reduce any further expense or legal exposure. He would kill Mr. Rebele at the school where he was an assistant principal and frame Danny. Later he would kill Danny and eliminate both his problems.

Meanwhile, the administrator's brother, this same Mr. Rebele, had been causing the senior class of the public school so much trouble that the class's teacher, former Judge David Howell, was convening a mock court of inquiry to find the source of the senior class's problems. Mr. Rebele had had Christopher falsely arrested as a gang member and had framed his friend Bobby for the natural death of an English teacher. He was damaging Adam as well.

As soon as his name appeared on the posted list of witnesses for the court of inquiry , Mr. Rebele announced, "I just might not be available to testify at this little court of inquiry."

Truer words were never spoken, but it was not his reluctance to tell the truth that nearly prevented his appearance but a child named Alice, her lunchbox, and a bullet.

The murder of the obnoxious assistant principal was spectacularly unsuccessful because of a fifth grader named Alice who had a serious grudge and a heavy, gold brick she had borrowed.

Years ago Alice was removed from her mother after a nearly fatal, intentional injury which left her with a pronounced limp, very thick glasses, and an unyielding law and order attitude. That put her on a collision course with Mr. Rebele, who called her Snow White when no one was around because of her beautiful black skin.

Alice had been adopted by the person who had nursed her back to health following her injury. Her adoption took place in Judge Howell's court, but fortunately did not involve the Rebele's adoption agency. She knew of her friend Danny's adoption a few years later by the evil Mr. Stack, arranged by the Rebeles in a distant county.

Meanwhile, the court of inquiry had come to the attention of Judge Howell's acquaintances and to the attention of the judiciary, District Judge Villa ordered a legally constituted Court of Inquiry to see why the senior class was being illegally threatened with not graduating and to see who was behind this. Judge Villa kept the same date and the same courtroom, that is, the classroom of former Judge David Howell.

The superintendent of the school district approved of the court even though his nephew, Mr. Rebele, was the cause of it. He told Mr. Rebele, "You will attend and testify unless you are dead."

Mr. Stack could not have summed things up more succinctly himself.

THE DAY
OF COURT

Almost nothing about the day of the court of inquiry was what was expected. The entire senior class thought the assistant principal who caused the court to be convened would hide and not testify. Everyone thought he would plead illness since he had been attacked and shot.

The death of the beloved English teacher was found to have been from natural causes, not murder and would not be investigated further. The tasteless note left beside her body claiming murder was mentioned in the affidavit of the detective who resolved her death but would not be pursued and her death would not be part of the proceedings except to show the note writer's malice.

Even the judge presiding over the court was not the retired judge who taught the class or even the district judge who had legally convened this court of inquiry. A court reporter from a district court downtown had set up her stenographer's machine at the front of the classroom and began typing as the armed bailiff also borrowed from the courthouse announced, "This Court of Inquiry for the 34th Judicial District of the State of Texas having been posted and the witnesses having been subpoenaed as required by law is now called to order, the Honorable Kathleen Gonzalez presiding."

Retired Judge Howell recalled being present many years ago when Kathleen had given her first magistrate's warning to a group of young men who were charged with a drive-by shooting. She told them their rights and set their bonds and then explained to them as if they were children, that they could not go home, that they had to stay in the jail that night because they had tried to kill someone. She asked if they understood. Several cried. David Howell thought she was teaching them as much as anyone ever could.

"Today, young ladies and gentlemen, is filled with surprises. Retired Judge David Howell, your teacher, began this exercise to discover why you were being threatened with not graduating. Then Judge Villa was to have conducted today's court, but he is finishing a murder trial, and so, as the law allows, I was invited to take his place here today.

"The magistrates take turns being on call, making findings of probable cause or no probable cause for persons arrested and brought before the magistrate, setting bonds, determining indigency and reading these persons their rights. I was on call throughout last night but in between those calls, I reviewed everything to do with today's hearing. In case you are worried, I am prepared and want you to know that the council of judges takes this court and your futures most seriously although, at your request, today's hearing will be completed within one hour unless something new is added.

"Some of the matters that were to have been considered today will be resolved by affidavits or offers of proof. Several new matters following testimony will almost assuredly be referred to a grand jury for indictments. Federal violations, if any, will be referred to the U.S. Attorney represented here today.

"One of your classmates will be the presenter of facts. He will also elicit information from the witnesses. He will be assisted by Attorney Stanley from the U.S. Attorney's office as I mentioned because there are possible federal violations. Your presenter is also assisted by Ms. Howard of the district attorney's office. To avoid violating state bar rules, the court will accept the stipulation that Mr. Carmine Shields is not practicing law, but is practicing practicing law. Mr. Shields."

"Thank you, judge. This morning, unless other crimes come up, we will cover: the death of Ms. Sanchez, an English teacher, the threat of this class not graduating, allegations of all crimes committed by this class, one allegation of a crime committed by a fifth grader, and finally the attempted murder of Mr. Rebele.

"The first witness is Detective David Lambchild. Sir, have been sworn in and you are being asked to take the chair here beside the American flag. As the court is well aware, but for the education of my classmates, I point out that the rule has not been invoked meaning the witnesses will be allowed to remain in the courtroom and hear the other witnesses' testimony unless the court chooses to invoke the rule."

The judge indicated her agreement with the current arrangement and looked at former Judge Howell to indicate how well she thought Carmine had been instructed.

"Detective, can you tell us about the death of Ms. Sanchez?"

"Ms. Sanchez was under the care of a heart doctor who states in his affidavit that her death was not unexpected. She was found at her desk by her students. Her heart medication was in her purse. There was a note found under her hand suggesting she had been killed, but if it was put there before she died, while she slept, it would be simply an attempt at humor. A suggestion was made that a particular member of this class should be suspected of killing her, but that idea was found to be completely without merit."

"Did your chief order you to look into any criminal activity of this class?"

"Yes. All criminal activity. There were allegations of gang membership, illegal possession of a firearm, theft of a firearm, carrying of a firearm on the prohibited premises of this school, possession and sale of narcotics at a school, and criminal trespass on private property, all of this against one student. All charges were unfounded.

"There is one student who is on probation for drug charges who is attending drug counseling and who is in compliance with his probation requirements. He was re-arrested one evening for failure to report. The probation office had been closed due to a gas leak and this alleged violation was reviewed by a justice of the peace and the student's probation and personal recognizance bond were reinstated. Afterwards, this student's bond was raised to $30,000.00 at the insistence of the assistant principal. An attorney cash bond has been posted."

"May this witness be excused subject to being recalled after other testimony?"

"Yes. and do I understand that your next witness, Mr. Bobby Omara, will no longer need to testify?"

"Yes, your honor." She had known him since he was a child since she served on the board of the Center where he lived. She was impressed that he had even survived.

"It is nice to see you again, Bobby."

"Thank you, judge. It is nice to see you, too. And if I am allowed to say, even though you've been on duty all night, you look beautiful."

"Baby, to look this good you've got to get up early."

No one at the school could be surprised that Bobby knew everyone in the city, but even former Judge Howell was very impressed with how much he was cherished.

"The next witness is Mr. Rebele, but I do not see my final witness, Alice."

Just then David's cell phone vibrated. He stepped out of the classroom and heard Alice's voice. "Lambchild, this is Alice. Mr. Stack will try to kill Danny, the boy he adopted, right now and he will try to make it look like Mr. Rebele did it to get even. He thinks Mr. Rebele will be hiding from Judge Howell's court. I saw Mr. Stack shoot Mr. Rebele by the reflexion in Mr. Rebele's glasses. Don't worry. Christopher and I will take care of Danny. We are going to Danny's house."

David had received more than a few terrifying phone calls over the years as an officer and as a detective, but this one was pretty near the top. He raced out of the school and notified dispatch to be on the lookout for a very large, very clean, very old Chrysler Newport, beige in color. Its occupants needed protection. He texted Judge David Howell and told him he hoped to bring Alice to testify within the hour.

Meanwhile Alice was riding in style in the back seat of that old, luxurious Chrysler, speaking to Christopher, the driver, and to his front seat passenger, Danny, as they drove slowly to where Danny lived. They were the only three on the planet who knew what was about to happen with the exception of Mr. Stack who thought he knew and David Lambchild who knew what might happen.

Danny had called Mr. Stack and said he was on his way home to his caregivers. Mr. Stack met the car in the driveway and aimed a pistol through the windshield at Danny. He thought he also had plenty of time to shoot the driver and then the little girl who had messed up his attempt to kill Mr. Rebele.

He was an excellent shot but when Mr. Keeling, the original Chrysler owner, said he had strengthened the windshield with the help of his deputy friend, he really meant it. Mr. Stack emptied the pistol with only lead smears and gunpowder residue appearing on the bullet resistant windshield.

As this was still happening, David arrived and handcuffed Mr. Stack and told him his rights and put him in the back of the detective's car. Mr. Stack appeared deflated and offered no resistance. David could not help himself; he said to them, "You are very brave, but you endangered your lives and we have no proof of what he has done."

Alice said in what might have been a sarcastic tone, "Oh, you mean like...a dash cam."

David thought, Devil's child but did not say it. He also thought about what would have happened if the evil Mr. Stack had shot through the side windows.

There was barely time to get back to the court of inquiry.

The very humbled and slow moving Mr. Rebele had testified standing because the graze down most of his back hurt most when he sat. He admitted putting the note under Ms. Sanchez' hand and blaming Bobby when he heard she was dead. He admitted his law and order agenda had unfairly damaged the school and this class in particular. Specifically, he apologized to Bobby, and to Adam and to Christopher. He testified that he had submitted his resignation to his uncle, the superintendent, before coming to school today, and his uncle had accepted it.

He told the court that he and his sister were shutting down their adoption agency and cooperating fully with the federal investigators.

By this time, no one in the temporary courtroom doubted anything he said and believed him when he said he had no clear memory of what happened when he was shot and only remembered a great pain in his right leg and then a searing pain down the back of his head and down his back.

Mr. Rebele was excused from the witness stand just as Alice made her entrance and marched with a most pronounced limp to the witness chair.

Miss Howard, from the district attorney's office, asked permission of the court to speak and announced that no charges would be brought against Alice for her lunchbox assault against Mr. Rebele since rather surprisingly no one witnessed it. Her testimony was more valuable to the d.a.'s office than a Class A assault conviction anyway, so Alice was given immunity. She had the assistant d.a. sign the agreement and then was sworn in. Mr. Rebele had signed a nonprosecution statement partly because he was confused about what happened and partly because he now knew that Alice had saved his life although certainly not on purpose.

Carmine Shields resumed questioning, noting for the class and court that they were still on schedule to finish within the allotted hour. Detective Lambchild had to bring Mr. Stack with him to get Alice back in time and had handcuffed him to a radiator in the hallway outside the classroom.

"Alice McCall, you are here to testify about the attempted murder."

"Which one?"

Carmine took a very deep breath and looked at former Judge Howell and then at Judge Gonzalez and then back at Alice. In the time it took him to exhale slowly he decided three things and proceeded to act upon them.

"Alice, can you tell us how you recovered from your injury?"

"When I got out of the hospital I went into a foster home. My foster parent was a nurse and had to keep my head bandaged because it was still swollen. There was a drain tube that had to be kept clean. I could not get glasses until the swelling went down. Without these glasses I am almost completely blind. Bobby from the center would come by every evening and walk with me and called himself my seeing eye boy. We walked a little more every evening until I got my strength. We made a trade. I would tell him when what he saw was not real and he would tell me when I could walk a little more. That is when I decided to go to religion classes with him and Christopher after my Baptist services each Sunday to see where he learned to be that way."

Carmine's first step was to let everyone especially the judge know Alice a little bit. He wanted the class and court to know she was sane. That was done.

"Now, Alice will you tell us about when Mr. Rebele was shot?"

She held the d.a.'s agreement in her hand and barely glanced at it. But she did glance at it. "I took the gold brick Mr. Rebele uses as his doorstop and put it in my lunchbox. I did not learn this in religion class or at my church. I followed him to the classroom and when he was facing me, I hit him with my lunchbox as hard as I could above his right ankle. He yelled in pain and fell on me just when I heard the gunshot. His face was very close to mine and I could see the reflection of that nasty Mr. Stack in his right glasses lens. He seemed confused about why Mr. Rebele had landed on me and had not died. I saw Mr. Stack put the pistol in his waist and cover it with his coat and leave." He wanted her off the hook for the assault. Done.

"Alice, in these few weeks with Judge Howell we have been taught that attorneys do not usually ask a question without knowing the answer. We have also been taught when to trust goodness. So, Alice. You mentioned other attempted murders. Can you tell us about them?"

"Yes. Mr. Stack tried to shoot Danny and me and Christopher, the disciple, a few minutes ago in Christopher's car. He brought the dash cam to prove it. He gave it to Lambchild."

"Why do you call him by his last name?"

"That's his name. That's what the chief calls him, too."

"Your honor."

"Thank you, Mr. Shield. That concludes this Court's business. The state and federal attorneys present will receive copies of today's transcript and of the dash cam from the court reporter and will proceed as they see fit.

"This Court of Inquiry stands adjourned."